WAR O

The car had been blo far and wide. The nearest two cars of the string ahead of it lay on their sides, their loads spilled on the ground. Suddenly, unexpectedly, a volley of rifle fire seared through the hazy smoke. Bullets ripped by Jessie, mere inches away.

Hugging the earth under a six-wheel wagon, Jessie searched for the source of the attack. Eighteen, perhaps twenty, riders were streaming in to strike from the rear. Concentrating their lethal mayhem on the workers trapped in the middle, they poured in salvos, bullets riddling tools and equipment.

The man beside Jessie grunted and collapsed. She wormed his old, battered Winchester out of his grasp and lost no time picking up where he'd left off, instantly dropping a rider out of his saddle. She rolled, levering, to find another—while their assailants continued to swarm . . .

WESLEY ELLIS

LONE STAR AND THE STEEL RAIL SELLOUT

JOVE BOOKS, NEW YORK

LONE STAR AND THE STEEL RAIL SELLOUT

A Jove Book / published by arrangement with
the author

PRINTING HISTORY
Jove edition / August 1993

ISBN: 0-515-11167-8

Jove Books are published by The Berkley Publishing Group,
200 Madison Avenue, New York, New York 10016.
The name "JOVE" and the "J" logo
are trademarks belonging to Jove Publications, Inc.

PRINTED IN THE UNITED STATES OF AMERICA

10 9 8 7 6 5 4 3 2 1

★

Chapter 1

The town was called Flush, and Jessie felt right away in her bones that it was a bad town—the kind she usually tried to stay clear of. But for anyone riding across California's central desert country north of the Salton Sea, the town meant welcome food and lodging. So, in that sense, she decided Flush didn't look like a really dangerous town—but then, bad towns rarely did.

Good or bad, there wasn't much, and nothing too prosperous. A main street, crosshatched sidestreets, dung-littered alleys, and about thirty buildings: decrepit saloons, stores, and hovel-sized homes. Roughly midway on one side of the street was a livery stable, and on the other side was the only hotel, a two-story false-front sticking up like a festering thumb from a row of one-story shops, its patch-painted siding looking like scrap lumber from some old dance hall. An arch over the entrance read, EL CENTRO INN.

To a great degree, Jessie and Ki appeared to fit their grubby surroundings. Slumped wearily on the spring seat of their wagon, both wore well-worn jeans and denim jackets, dusty woolen shirts and sweat-stained, flop-brimmed hats. Jessie did not appear to be what she really was: a proud, aristocratic woman in her mid-twenties; a crack shot with her now-holstered pistol or the twin-shot derringer concealed behind her wide belt buckle; and a shrewd, knowledgeable heiress to immense wealth, the Starbuck international business empire. Nor did Ki seem to be more than a tall, lean man in his early thirties, of mixed Japanese and Caucasian blood, and so peaceful by nature that he lacked a gunbelt or any other sign of a firearm. In fact, though, he was a samurai-trained master of martial arts, in whose old leather vest were secreted short daggers and similar small throwing weapons, including razor-edged, star-shaped steel disks called *shuriken*.

Despite their own needs, the welfare of their horses came first with the two travelers. Ki reined in the wagon in front of the livery barn, and Jessie paid the hostler twenty dollars in advance for a single night's grooming and graining for the team. The wagon was what was known as a farmer's canopy-top surrey, only this one had had its rear seat removed to make room for Jessie's bulky wardrobe trunks. From the pile of trunks, Ki extracted his small gladstone bag and Jessie's small traveling case and with Jessie started across to the El Centro. Originally, many years back, Ki had come from Japan to San Francisco, the black-haired, almond-eyed, bronze-complected man having been hired by Jessie's father. Consequently, he and Jessie had virtually grown up together, and after Alex Starbuck was murdered, it seemed only fitting for Ki to continue with her as her confidant and protector. As affectionate and trusting as any blood brother and sister, they made a formidable team.

"I've seen mangier hotels," Ki observed, "but rarely."

"It's only for tonight," Jessie replied, sounding more optimistic than she felt. The El Centro was definitely a comedown from the luxurious hacienda of her father's old friend Thurlow Whitworth, owner of sprawling Rancho Dorado to the west, where she and Ki had just spent a week's vacation. Tucking a stray wisp of coppery-blond hair up under her hat, Jessie cast Ki a hopeful smile, and despite the exhausting effects of their journey, the evening chill could not dampen the warmth of her sultry face, with its high cheekbones, audacious green eyes, and the provocative quirk of her lips. "Besides, tomorrow night we'll have to camp out. Day after, we'll reach Indio and catch the Southern Pacific and be on our way back to the Circle Star," she added, already looking forward to being home again at her Starbuck headquarters and ranch in Texas.

The El Centro was more depressing inside than out, its lobby mobbed, as were its restaurant and saloon. Jessie and Ki managed to press in and rent rooms, with bath privileges down the hall. Then they pushed to the restaurant, where they waited long for a table and longer for their orders. They spent their time observing the horde around them and in the more boisterous and rowdy saloon, which was nearby, through an open connecting door. The patrons were a mix of ages and types, mostly ranchers and hands and their ilk, but some wore garb of the country south of the border.

Eventually the waiter came with their food. As he was serving, a raucous shout burst from the saloon, drawing their attention.

A big, florid-faced American, dressed in all the flashy finery of a Californio don, was leaning across the bar, the elbows of his blue velvet jacket on the counter. A broad-brimmed vicuña hat was pushed to the back of his greasy black hair. A red sash banded his thick middle above the black line of his slanting gunbelt. Gold-embroidered, tight-fitting *calzónera* breeches hugged his sturdy legs. He was yelling at the barkeep and making pawing motions for another bottle of whiskey, which the barkeep was hurriedly bringing.

"The gent looks like he just came from a drunken fandango," Jessie remarked. "Why else would an American be wearing such a fancy foofaraw outfit?"

"Yeah, the outfit would be better suited for the guy next to him," Ki said. That man, a peon by his looks and tattered clothes, was a little hombre wearing a floppy cone-peaked straw sombrero that sagged almost to his shoulders. Ki's glance swung curiously to study the rest of the bar patrons, and his dark eyes narrowed a little as he regarded three men seated at a poker table just in front of the *paisano* and the big American.

He pointed them out to Jessie. The three were lean-bodied, hard-faced, all cut from the same mold. A certain coyote-like tightness about them tabbed them for Ki and Jessie as renegades, either in off the desert or down from San Bernardino. Toying with drinks that didn't seem to interest them, the trio kept their agate eyes on that narrow-shouldered peon in the droopy sombrero.

Their interest in the tattered little peon was peculiar enough, but not half so surprising to Jessie and Ki as the look that crossed the peon's brown face when he turned his head and happened to spot the two of them sitting in the restaurant. The man's eyes widened. Then his white teeth gleamed in a smile.

"Señor Ki!" His voice carried sharply across the barroom hubbub. "Señor Ki, Señorita Starbuck! *Mes amigos! Por Dios,* I am glad to see you again. Come, come and drink with your old frien' Jimenez Raul Linares!"

Jimenez Raul Linares. Friend, the peon had called them. Jessie and Ki glanced at each other, startled, although their expressions were bland, unreadable. They hoped their features were telling that trio and the fine-feathered gringo nothing, for they were conscious suddenly that all four men were watching them with thinly veiled interest. So was the thin-faced peon, whom they had never seen before, a pleading in his eyes.

For some reason, the flashy hombre and the three gunmen were watching that peon like cats about to pounce on a mouse. Just why, Jessie did not know, but she made up her mind that it might be worth her while to find out. Or rather, Ki's while—as a lady, it would have been improper for her to go into the saloon, but Ki could, and did. As if reading Jessie's mind, he stood up, put his napkin on the table, and forced a smile to his lips.

"Jimenez!" he exclaimed, and started forward, across the hard plank floor, one hand extended.

"Damned if this isn't a surprise meeting you here. How come you're in Flush?"

The look of relief that Ki saw pass swiftly across Linares's face was enough reward for whatever help he might render the little peon. Linares stepped away from the bar with a lithe, catlike grace that spoke of silken muscles beneath the shabby garb he wore. No muscle-bound Mex workman ever had that kind of stride. His was the proud, effortless walk of a hidalgo. The fineness of his clean-cut features spoke of breeding, too. It came to Ki—and to Jessie behind him—that the shabby peon rated the *charro* garb of the gringo far more than its wearer. That knowledge tautened Ki's and Jessie's nerves and brought with it a tingle of excitement. There was a mystery here that needed solving. Danger, too, but they had never turned away from that.

Ki and the peon were together now, a few feet from the scarred counter where the gringo watched them. Linares's teeth were still gleaming in that welcoming smile as he sidestepped Ki's extended hand and threw his arms about him in a fervent Latin embrace.

"Ah amigo!" Linares's words were loud in Ki's ears. "I had never hoped to see you here!"

Ki felt something small, hard, and heavy drop into one of his vest pockets, and words barely louder than the sound of an exhaled breath touched his ears.

"Carry this token for me to the Cantina Cara Dura, señor, and it will mean more to Señorita Starbuck than her load of finery in your wagon!"

The peon's voice grew instantly loud again in chattering comment about his pleasure at seeing Señor

Ki again, only this time Ki wasn't listening. He was thinking about the Cantina Cara Dura as Linares, with an arm about his waist, propelled him to the bar, calling to the bartender to bring fresh glasses and a bottle. With slender, strong fingers the peon poured and raised his glass to "old friend" Ki.

"Salud, amigo," he cried. "We will drink, and then I must go, for the night grows short and I must return to El Pueblo de Los Angeles, our blessed City of Angels."

Playing the game, Ki tipped his glass. "Good luck," he said, and downed the drink. The cheap whiskey brought tears to his eyes and questions to his mind—questions that he dared not voice, for he could feel the drill-sharp eyes of the fancy-garbed gringo boring into his back, and he could see the three gunmen at the table watching him as closely now as they'd been watching the peon.

Jimenez Linares banged his glass on the bar and laid a fifty-dollar slug beside it. He stepped back and raised his hand airily to Ki. *"Buenas noches,* Ki," he said lightly. "Until we meet again, I will bid you a good night and a pleasant slumber." He headed out of the saloon, waving good-bye to a puzzled Jessie Starbuck on his way through the dining room.

The peon had almost reached the lobby entrance when Ki heard the scrape of chairs at the table where the three gunmen were seated. Out of the corner of his eye, he watched two of the threesome rise and stretch. With unconscious caution they hitched sagging gunbelts about their waists, and though he hadn't seen the beefy gringo at his back pass the signal, Ki felt suddenly certain that the *charro*-garbed *Americano* had ordered that pair to follow the peon.

This answered a question that had been plaguing Ki ever since Linares had dropped that hard object into his pocket. He had wondered then if any of this watchful quartet had seen the peon's action. Now he felt confident they hadn't, or else they wouldn't be stepping after Linares. Again exchanging glances with Jessie, he began moving to intercept that coyote-faced duo as they headed for the lobby door. This was none of his or Jessie's affair, a part of Ki's mind told him, but at the same time a more reckless section of his brain was telling him that they had been dealt cards in this strange game and had to play out their hand.

The narrow-eyed absorption of the pair stepping after Linares told Ki something more. The two men were after a kill. Once in the sheltering night outside the El Centro, a quick bullet or a thudding gun butt would end the peon's life, and Ki felt mortally certain that the thing in his pocket would be responsible for the killing. And though he could readily kill the two, that could very well suck him and Jessie into more trouble than it would cure. There had to be a better way . . .

With the suddenness of a man caught at last by one drink too many, Ki clutched at his flat stomach with both hands and doubled forward, retching violently. Like a man blinded by nausea, he staggered forward into the path of the men. His hunched shoulder caught one of them in the chest and sent him stumbling aside. The full weight of his body hit the other, and he sprawled sideward, against the hotel wall.

"Why, you fuckin' chink bastard!" the first man cursed savagely. The second man bounced back from the wall, and his long right arm lashed out cruelly.

The open-handed slap cracked solidly against Ki's jaw. Ki had seen the blow coming, but in his feigned drunkenness he dared not try and avoid it. The force of the slap jarred him to his heels, and he straightened.

"Damn you slant-eyes, you can't hold your likker!" the second man bellowed profanely. "Stay outta my way, or I'll put a bullet hole in you that'll drain out that rotgut you've been swillin'!"

Ki stood there, the mark of fingers on his cheek, and took the abuse with assumed glassy stupidity.

Steps were approaching. Ki heard them, and then he felt a hand clamp his shoulder and knew it belonged to the big gringo with the foofaraw rig. The man's voice was hearty when he spoke.

"Now, now, Turk." He addressed the second renegade cheerfully. "Take it easy. After all, we haven't always held our liquor. You and Merle go about your business. I'll take care of this. Sometimes one drink will tend to have a sobering effect when a gent's in your condition, Mr., er . . . Mr. Ki. Come on back to the bar and have one on me. After all, you should enjoy drinking with a real American more'n a damned greaser, even if he is a friend of yours."

A drunken swing of his head showed Ki that Linares had made good his escape. From now on, he told himself, the peon was on his own. "Greaser?" He let his head swing toward the beefy-faced, smooth-tongued gringo. "What greaser? I dunno any—"

"Bodeen!" The first renegade had recovered his breath. He came surging forward to clutch his leader's arm. "Look, Bodeen," he said hoarsely, "there ain't no sense in us trying to follow that damned Linares in the dark. We—"

"You'll do what I say, Merle." Bodeen's voice had the bite of a lash. "Get out, you two, and don't come back without—" He stopped abruptly and glanced at the stupid-looking Ki alongside him. "Did you say you don't know Linares?"

Ki bobbed his head drunkenly. "Linares?" he said thickly. "Dunno no Linares, no greaser."

Fine veins mapped Bodeen's full cheeks. They purpled as Ki watched the man. "Then get the hell outta here!" The gringo was holding his rage in check with an effort. "Damn you, I oughtta bend a gun barrel over your skull, but you probably wouldn't know what happened!"

Ki felt Bodeen's heavy hand catch at his jacket collar and twist him around. A boot rose and caught him accurately in the seat of the pants, and he stumbled down the boardwalk after the renegade duo. A quick glance either way showed him that both they and Linares had disappeared into the darkness.

Some hours later, after Ki and Jessie had met up again and then retired to their separate rooms, Jessie rose from her bed and lit the room's kerosene lantern. By its flickering light, she studied the object that the peon had slipped into Ki's vest pocket.

When Ki had taken it out of his pocket and given it to her, they had seen that it was an odd, flat coin a bit larger than a silver dollar—a coin made even stranger by the fact that it was cut in half. Now, inspecting the coin for details, Jessie saw the lamplight glow like a red coal over the face of the metal. The coin was gold, solid gold, she guessed, and it had been hammered from a single great nugget. Perhaps an eighth of an inch thick, the coin had a smooth surface that was scored with an intricate mass of lines. Infinite time and patience had gone into the engraving of this gold piece. Delicately done, time had worn the lines smooth.

When whole, the coin had been a collector's object of infinite worth, Jessie realized as she studied it. Thinking of that got her thinking of the Cantina Cara Dura, where Jimenez Linares had wanted them to take the coin. Thirty miles west of Calexico, virtually on the Mexican border, a tangled, fantastic maze of buttes towered toward the colorless California sky. It was an area where anyone could get lost in a tangle of badlands that even the Devil wouldn't claim. And right in the heart of that desert a man as fantastic as the country surrounding him had built the Cantina Cara Dura, which loosely translated meant Tavern of the Cheek of the Devil. Jessie had never been there. Few honest folk had, she knew, for there was nothing on that desert to attract them. Certainly not *El Cochino,* keeper of the Cara Dura.

Little was known about *El Cochino,* The Gross One. Rumor claimed that any man on the dodge from San Bernardino to the border could seek refuge at his tavern, if he had the price. And the price, oddly enough, was in many cases no more than a rare coin. An ancient doubloon or silver piece, it was said, could unlock the elephant's heart quicker than a poke of dust. For *El Cochino* was known to have in his tavern the most fabulous backbar of any in California. Behind the glass panels that surrounded a central mirror his coin collection had been arranged to catch the eyes of all who might enter. A thing of beauty and uncounted value, it was the pride and delight of the three-hundred-pound giant who ruled the desert badlands and the Cara Dura.

And thinking of the Cantina Cara Dura got Jessie to thinking of a peculiar coincidence: Roughly a dozen miles north of the tavern, the Mexicali & San Diego Railroad was laying track. The M&SD was a subsidiary of Jessie's Starbuck Transportation, a division of her Starbuck Enterprises; and, as its name implied, the rail line was being built to link the Mexican railway terminus at Mexicali with coastal Southern California at San Diego. According to the latest report Jessie had received, construction had progressed west by northwest from Mexicali as far as an end-of-track town called Lobos. And from here at Flush, she could strike almost due south and reach Lobos and then continue straight on to hit Cantina Cara Dura.

Thinking of the railroad made Jessie think of the troubles incurred by its construction. Every project had problems and railroading often had more than its share, but in the case of the M&SD, to the granite forces of nature had been added the difficulties posed by man. First, some distance west of Lobos was Blister River, where the best crossing point was controlled by a contrary, moonshine-peddling old reprobate named White Water Whittaker, who was refusing to negotiate a right-of-way with the railroad. Second, the Adams Stage Line, which hauled between Mexicali and San Diego, had a control clause in its California state charter:

> . . . And that furthermore the operator, his heirs and assigns, shall for a period of fifteen years have full and exclusive rights to carry passenger traffic within the legal bounds of Imperial

and San Diego Counties as established on Map Number 393 Page . . .

Considering that Imperial County bordered Mexicali, and that San Diego County abutted Imperial, this meant the M&SD was off-limits by a matter of nine years in attempting to tap the heavy freight and passenger traffic between Mexico and the West Coast.

On top of such legal entanglements, the M&SD was also running into criminal opposition—trains were being wrecked, buildings burned, camps raided, jobs bungled, machinery sabotaged. According to M&SD's general manager, Otis Delivan, blame for all this deliberate destruction fell on Tornado Turnbeau and his outlaw gang. Nicknamed for his deadly, whirlwind style of attack, Turnbeau preyed on the border region from his stronghold in the desolate Laguna Mountains. The proposed route of the M&SD would take it over the Lagunas, smack-dab through Turnbeau's territory, and evidently the outlaw chief saw the advent of the railroad as the coming of law and order.

To complicate matters further, much of that area was part of an ancient Spanish land grant. The grant was huge, well over a half million acres, incorporating not only a chunk of the Lagunas, but also most of the adjacent range, the even wilder Cuyamacas. Of course, the M&SD had to obtain a right-of-way to cross the grant lands, but so far no one could be found to give permission. In fact, the government land courts were threatening to open the grant lands for colonization unless the heirs of old Don Teran Fundador could produce the original grant signed by the King of Spain. If that should happen, gaining the necessary right-of-ways from a multitude of homesteaders and shirttail ranchers would be close to impossible.

The only alternative was to reroute the railroad in a long southern swing flanking the border, reaching San Diego up through Jamul Valley. Indeed, many of Jessie's advisors and all of M&SD's board of directors had recommended that route from the first, and had thrown up their hands in consternation when Jessie backed Delivan's decision to cut straight through, across the mountains and grant lands. But Jessie had great confidence in Delivan, or she wouldn't have picked him to be general manager, and she wasn't about to interfere with his authority then—or now. Besides, he had reached a frame of mind she knew well. He would listen to no reason, or what others thought was reason. No, Jessie had every intention of leaving him alone to do the job she'd hired him to do—and which if anyone could do, he could, out of sheer bullheaded tenacity.

So Jessie saw no value in making a side trip to Lobos. As for the Cantina Cara Dura, well . . . There was value in the half of the coin in her hand, Jessie reckoned. At least it was worth the wolf hunt four men were making for one scared little peon. And if they caught him, Jimenez Linares would die, and the flashy gringo, Bodeen, would learn that Linares did not have the coin. If Bodeen found that out, he'd start looking for Ki and Jessie. Thoughtfully she padded across to where her gunbelt was slung over the back of a chair, and removed her Colt pistol from its holster. Sighing, she put it and the coin beneath her pillow.

There was just one thing certain, Jessie decided as sleep caught up with her. She wasn't going to deliver the mutilated gold piece to the Cantina Cara Dura.

★

Chapter 2

Morning came, and stretched toward noon.

Behind the high-sided surrey lay the twisting wagon trail up along the eastern foothills of the Santa Rosas. Paused now to lunch and rest their team in the high notch of Octillo Grade, they let their eyes flicker backward down the hairpins of the road they had just traveled. Nothing moved across their line of vision, and for perhaps the fiftieth time since pulling out of Flush, Ki shook his head sadly. They were half a day out of the town, and they had seen no sign of Linares, or the gringo Bodeen and his renegade crew.

As hot as a coal against her breast, that mutilated coin lay in the pocket of Jessie's shirt. Not for an hour since she'd woken that morning had she been able to forget its presence. "The only thing I can figure," she told Ki, "is that Linares was on his way to the Cantina Cara Dura to try and peddle the coin to *El Cochino*."

"Maybe so, Jessie, but that doesn't explain the presence of Bodeen and his men. Bodeen looked like a man who's used to playing for high stakes, and that odd half-coin can't be worth more than a few hundred bucks to any collector. Certainly it isn't worth murder."

"You're right, it doesn't add up. Besides, if money was what Linares needed, why did he toss out a fifty-dollar gold piece to pay for a pair of drinks? And how'd he know our names? And where'd he and Bodeen's wolf pack disappear to?" Lips pursed, Jessie glanced down at the Winchester .44-40 carbine in its scabbard against the footboard. "I'd give plenty," she said, "to know if that bunch is waiting for us somewhere ahead."

The thought sent her glance forward. From this high vantage point she could see the vast, incredibly desolate stretch they had to cross to reach Indio, the sands refracting light like a shattered mirror. Almost reluctantly then, Jessie turned her gaze to the south, toward the ragged buttes banding the horizon on that side. Vermillion, indigo, and gold splashed those cliffs with incredible color. And beyond them some seventy miles or more lay the Cantina Cara Dura, as mysterious as the coin in her pocket.

Her jaw tightened grimly. "That's one place," she vowed, "where Jessica Starbuck isn't going!"

She was still in the same frame of mind when night caught them on the edge of the sands. They camped at an oasislike grove that fringed a water hole, staking the horses in a patch of straggly grass. After supper, Ki scattered the coals of their fire and they rolled up in their soogans under the surrey, fully dressed, weapons handy. They both preferred the discomfort of sleeping clad and armed whenever camping out in wild country, strangers in a strange land. The day had been long, hot, grueling, and they slept the sleep of exhaustion.

When Ki came awake sometime during the night hours, he realized that Jessie's concern over Linares and Bodeen must have pervaded his own dreams. It had been more of a nightmare, about a night marauder who had slipped into their camp and cut the picket ropes holding their team. Mounted on one of the horses, the cuss had then hazed the other one out along the rutted trail that led across the barren wasteland.

Telling himself it was nonsense, Ki reared from his soogan, able to look straight forward beneath the running gear of the surrey. The wagon trail stretched that way, shimmering white in the moonlight, and out along the ruts was moving the sudden reality of his dream. Two horses, heads held high to escape their dangling picket ropes, were streaming wildly into the desert. A lone, slender figure in a floppy, cone-peaked sombrero was hazing one along from the back of the other. Closer to camp, where the horses had been staked out, a hipshot mule stood tethered, and only now did it lift its head and bray mournfully.

Heartily Ki cursed as he rolled from the surrey. It wasn't enough that he'd let Jimenez Linares slip into camp and cut those picket lines. Now the mule Linares must have ridden in on was braying and spurring the peon into fast action.

Jessie, awakened by Ki's alarm, scrambled from beneath the wagon. Siltlike alkali was veiling the fleeing thief by the time she gained her feet, carbine in hand. Harsh barks from the peon were urging the horses into a run as he veered off the trail and headed southward. Jessie shouldered her carbine and then, finger on the trigger, held her fire. Close along the neck of his stolen horse, only the top of Linares's outlandish hat showed above the animal's ears. A target difficult to hit in daytime, it would be almost impossible in the moonlight and clouding alkali dust.

"More than likely all I'd do is plug one of the horses," she muttered to Ki. But she did send one shot over the head of the departing peon as Linares twisted and waved that floppy sombrero.

"Hasta la vista, Señorita Starbuck, Señor Ki!" Jimenez Linares's ironic call came floating back.

Ki stood there with his fists clenched. "Damn me! Linares doesn't want our horses any more than we want his damned busted gold piece. If he was hankering to set us afoot, he'd have taken his mule with him, too."

"He must've figured how I'd feel about visiting the Cantina of Cara Dura, and just aims to make sure we'll follow him," Jessie snapped, and then a grudging smile of admiration touched her lips. "Linares has guts, no denying that."

"And the stealth of an Apache," Ki allowed. "Y'know, despite all the trouble the little guy has got us into, I can't help feeling a liking for him, even though it looks like he's made us wild cards in whatever game he's playing."

"He won't feel like playing if I catch up with him," Jessie promised, eying the peon's hammerheaded old mule.

The gray, slatternly, flea-bitten animal had been groaning a plaintive accompaniment to Jessie and Ki's grumbling remarks, but now a snort that could mean only one thing came from its nostrils. The mule's head swung toward their backtrail. Lofty, gaunt in the night, the Santa Rosas loomed that way, blocking out the light of the westering moon.

They could see nothing as they tried to probe the night in the direction of the mountains. Ki's glance turned back to the mule just as it was bracing itself for a warning, or welcoming, bray. A long stride carried him to the mule's side, and grabbing the bridle rope in his left hand, he yanked down on it, cutting off the sound. Then, with Jessie bringing the carbine, Ki led the mule to the right, toward a cutbank wash that lay no more than a hundred feet from the grove. Company was coming, though it was still out of hearing.

"I hope they're beyond range of vision, too," Jessie commented, as she dipped into the cover of the dry wash. "If our visitors happen to be a bunch of horse-stealing Paiutes, we'll give them something to remember."

But their visitors were not Indians. They saw that for themselves fifteen minutes later, and Jessie levered the carbine as surprise narrowed her eyes.

Three riders had come from the shadows of the Santa Rosas and were cautiously approaching the stranded surrey. A stocky silhouette in the night, their leader wore a wide-brimmed hat set on the back of his head. The angle of the hat identified the man as Bodeen, the red-faced gringo with the smooth tongue who had been watching Linares in the El Centro.

Behind Bodeen rode the pair of coyote-faced renegades, Turk and Merle. As he recognized Turk, Ki's fingers rose to touch his jaw. It was still tender from the lashing blow the renegade had laid there. Jessie felt the hard weight of that broken coin in her pocket, and its mystery was a grim reminder that they had mixed in a blind and dangerous game.

Bodeen had reached the side of the surrey now. "Boys, this here's the wagon belongin' to the Starbuck bitch," they heard him exclaim loudly as he dismounted. "Hers and that damned drunk chink's who bumped you last night and let Linares escape."

A dry, mirthless chuckle came from the cougar-eyed Turk as he dismounted along with Merle. "This outfit ain't gonna be nothing but a pile of ashes when I get through with it," Turk growled. "Looks like Paiutes run off their horses, and they went chasin' 'em. We'll guide them back here by lightin' them a nice bonfire. It'll teach 'em, maybe, to mind their own business next time they mix with us."

"I ain't so sure yet," Merle chimed in, "that squint-eyed bastard was as drunk as he acted. Booze don't hit men so all-fired pronto."

"You're talking loco," Bodeen snarled, "and wasting time besides. We lost Linares, and now the best we can do is beat him to the Cara Dura. Meantime you'll burn no wagons, Turk. If we could steal it, that might be worthwhile, but even then we'd be playing penny ante."

Listening intently, in hopes that the talk of the three men might clear up the mystery of the coin Jessie was carrying, Ki had relaxed his grip on the mule's rope. A mistake. The mule's bray shattered the quiet of the night like a blast from Gabriel's trumpet.

At the sudden sound, they saw the trio jerk around like puppets attached to a string, and they knew that they'd be in trouble pronto unless they got the jump on it. Boldly Ki set the mule against the sloping bank of the cut wash and slapped it with the rope, and the mule went up the bank like a goat. As it lurched into view of the three men, Ki suddenly whirled—then froze.

"Uh-huh, don't move," a voice snarled from the shadows.

From the encircling rocks stepped another man—the third renegade in Bodeen's crew, the one who had taken no part in that drunk scene Ki had staged for their benefit. He was wearing grubby, nondescript work clothes and down-at-the-heel boots, and was covering Jessie and Ki with an old but well-cared-for Remington .44 revolver. "Drop your rifle, lady. Now, both of you start walking."

Marched out of the cut wash at gunpoint, Jessie and Ki saw the others draw their revolvers. And all of them looked ready, in fact downright eager, to kill with them.

"Hello!" Jessie called. "We're certainly glad to see you, whoever you may be." That was to make them think she was either a ditzy dame or nearsighted. "Yessir, very glad. Some bunch sneaked into camp a half hour or so ago and sliced our picket ropes. We followed and managed to rope this old lop-eared crowbait."

They had crossed the distance separating them from the men as Jessie talked, and now they stopped, facing the trio across a space of some ten feet. They noticed that the hatchet-thin Turk had an expression of wicked malice on his gaunt face.

"Only one hombre," Turk said, "run off your team, and it warn't no Paiute. They work in bunches." Gesturing with his revolver, he told Jessie, "Now, real easy, lady, out with your gun."

Using just the tips of her fingers, Jessie carefully drew her revolver and tossed it aside. Then she folded her hands in front of her, along her belt, tucking her thumbs behind the buckle. She glared, silent and defiant, at the surrounding hard-faced renegades.

Ki, however, was cringing. His lean, muscular body slumped pathetically as he whined, "Seems like I recollect meetin' you before. Also seems like I was drunk, and that you took advantage of it to lay one on me. Now I ain't hankering to have any trouble with you—"

"Shaddup." The third gunman eyed Ki up and down, then sneered mockingly, "Ain't got no gun, Chinee-boy?"

"No guts to use one," Merle quipped snidely.

"Betcha he's got somethin'. All them Chinks got hatchets and stuff hidden on 'em." Turk swaggered up to Ki and snickered. "In his vest, I betcha. You, take off your vest. Take off all your clothes."

"You best strip too, ma'am," Bodeen said to Jessie. "Now, we ain't interested in your surrey or trunks," he added placatingly. "We're out here looking for a thief that's stolen something from me that I value mighty heavily. Obviously he dropped in on y'all. We just can't take no chances on what he might've done with my property."

The beefy Bodeen was still wearing his gold-laced *calzónera* breeches and fancy blue jacket. He still looked like a foofaraw dude, except for his drill-sharp eyes. Those eyes, however, in Jessie's opinion, and his slippery tongue, made him the most dangerous of the group. And another things was obvious to her, and to Ki: Bodeen and his men had come for more than the coin. They had come for blood and mayhem, and weren't going to leave Jessie or Ki alive to blab about it.

"Sure, sure, anything you say," Ki said grovelingly, fumbling with the buttons of his vest. "Just don't hurt me. You won't hurt me, will you?"

The men laughed contemptuously.

As Jessie began removing her jacket, the third man said, "Hey, Merle, you wanna have a little fun with her first?"

Covering Jessie, Merle nodded. "She looks like a mighty tasty filly."

Turk guffawed. "They all look good to you. You ain't got no taste, that's your trouble." He raised his long-barreled revolver and aimed it straight at Ki's forehead. "I'm gonna do you a favor, boy. I'm gonna make a big, round eye smack dab in the middle of your two squinty slits."

It was the last move he made. Ki dove into action, springing across the short distance. Before Turk could squeeze the trigger, Ki struck with a *mae-geri-keage*—a forward snap-kick—followed by a *yoko-hija-ate*—sideways elbow smash—to cave in the man's ribs and stop his heart. Simultaneously he snapped a *shuriken* speeding toward Merle, who was alongside Jessie.

In the split second it took Ki to attack, Jessie flattened herself to the ground, glimpsing the *shuriken* as it sliced into Merle's throat. She knew that Ki, a proud and courageous fighter, loathed even to feign cowardice unless it was absolutely necessary to lull suspicion and gain a better position; seeing him groveling, she'd prepared herself to respond the instant he moved. Now, rolling, she came up with the twin-shot derringer in her right hand.

The remaining gunman, not so prepared, was triggering lead in a haphazard if concerted roar, trying to kill the not-so-defenseless Oriental. But Ki was not there. Springing again, Ki lashed out with a leaping kick, catching the man in the solar plexus. Clutching his hemmorhaging belly, the man fell to his knees, mimicking Merle, who'd crumpled hunched over as though he were praying, the *shuriken* protruding from his blood-spurting larynx.

And Jessie blew a hole through the chest of Bodeen before he could target Ki in his gun sights. Breathless, she regained her feet. Ki, seeing that she was all right, gave her a quick, slightly sad smile and went to retrieve his *shuriken* so as not to leave the unique evidence behind.

"Shouldn't have killed them," he murmured.

Jessie, patting her clothes free of dirt, sighed. "Don't regret it. I don't."

"At least one of them, Jessie. I should've held back, kept one alive to ask a few questions." He paused, shrugged. "Well, it can't be helped. What's done is done."

"And once done, one moves on. What now?"

"Exactly that. We've lost the mule but gained three horses. Four, if we can find where that fourth gent left his mount. So we can hitch up the surrey and find ourselves a safer place to camp. Where to then is up to you."

"No question about that. Señor Jimenez Raul Linares wanted us to follow him, and I sure and certain will. Straight down to Hell if his tracks go that far—only I fear they'll head toward that Cantina Cara Dura, and I'm not so sure but what that place is worse!"

★

Chapter 3

Pushing hard, Jessie and Ki reached Lobos four days later. Back when they had driven the surrey to Indio, Jessie had telegraphed Otis Delivan to expect their arrival in due course; she anticipated only a short layover, however, figuring that Jimenez Linares had surely passed Lobos by now and was heading south to the Cantina Cara Dura. Still, her wire to Delivan had been fairly lengthy, for two reasons: First, she was not about to admit her real motive for coming, but didn't want to send a message so brief and terse that it implied she was mad at Delivan and was visiting to kick butt. And second, she had a couple of notions about the real problems that were plaguing Delivan and the M&SD, and she wanted him to be prepared to discuss them when they met. Not surprising to her, knowing Delivan's can-do-now character, a detailed reply was waiting for her en route at the telegrapher's in the town of Brawley.

Although it was just shortly after dawn when Jessie and Ki rode into Lobos, the main street was already black with men, as was typical of a bustling end-of-track town. Also typical were the rows of frail, weather-blistered tar-paper shacks erected by the grading crews before the arrival of the rails—standing insults to every wind that blew. The same long piles of corded ties, the flimsy cabins and tents, the same canvas saloons and honkatonks thrown up overnight. The same sounds. The same stinks. It wasn't sweet. But it was railroad.

Jessie inhaled deeply, smelling the full smell of Lobos, soaking it all in. And her eye was taken by a pretentious unpainted structure that fronted the tracks. Its mammoth spread of canvas roofs covered an area a city block square, and the building itself was constructed in segments and panels joined together with wooden pegs, easy to set up and dismantle, obviously designed by someone who took the end-of-track business seriously. A sign over the swinging front doors identified it as the BELLE OF LOBOS. The word "Lobos" appeared to have been hastily painted over other names—no doubt the names of previous end-of-track towns in which the establishment had been erected.

Days earlier, back at Indio, Jessie and Ki had delivered the dead gunmen and their mounts to the sheriff, then shipped Jessie's trunks to Texas on the Southern Pacific, and traded in the wagon at the Indio livery for two saddle horses—a rambunctious bay mare and a deep-brisketed pinto gelding. Now, having ridden up the street a ways, they dismounted at a large canvas barn resembling a circus tent, across whose front was scribbled, Shamrock Livery Stable. Horses Groomed & Grained, $15.00 Per Day.

Jessie, aghast at the price, told the hostler, "I see not all the thieves wear guns!"

The hostler, a toothless geezer, cackled at her outraged expression. "Feed comes high. Everything has to be freighted in. You wanna pay for these two now, or add 'em to your bill?"

"Bill? What bill?"

"You is Miz Starbuck, ain'tcha?"

"Well, yes, but—"

"Thought so. Your Mexican wrangler described you both to a tee when he dropped off them two other horses of yours. Said you'd be along soon to square the bill."

"Linares!" Jessie swallowed thickly, part in surprise, part to control her temper. "Did he rent another saddler and charge it to me?"

"Nope, not from me anyhows." The hostler gave them a rheumy-eyed once-over, then opined: "You hit Lobos at a good time. T'day is payday, and everybody's celebrating, so you can join right in and celebrate your honeymoonin'. If there's anything I admire is a young married couple."

"Honeymooning! We're not married, I'll have you know," Jessie spat.

"Wal, that's accordin' to your wrangler." The hostler cackled again. "But if'n you're just skylarkin', I admire that even more."

Casting the hostler a look of mayhem, Jessie turned and stalked off. Ki followed, carrying their traveling bags. The hostler slapped his knee and hooted.

Walking back toward the hotel, Jessie and Ki could see that, as the hostler had mentioned, Lobos was gearing up for payday. Already the saloons were doing a good business, although it was nothing compared to what would come later in the day, when the pay car arrived and they began handing out packets of cash to the construction workers. Shopkeepers stood in their open doorways, alert and expectant. Dance-hall girls gathered in groups, chattering noisily, their too-bright eyes gleaming with anticipation, too-ready smiles on their too-red lips. Sprinkled among the crowed were waxy-faced gamblers and promoters, and the dregs of human flotsam and jetsam that followed the railroad terminus like flies follow a gut wagon. Saints and sinners—all going the same direction. Following the Glory Road to riches or to ruin.

Crossing the street to the hotel, Jessie and Ki went around a twenty-mule string team, hitched to three wagons laden with gravel for ballast. The heavily bearded driver stood beside his saddled near-wheeler, drinking from a huge stone jug and bellowing ribald comments to passersby. Jessie and Ki ignored his taunts and entered the Belle of Lobos.

Signing the register, Jessie said to the clerk, "I'm looking for Mr. Delivan of Mexicali & San Diego."

"One-oh-eight. But he's gone out already."

"You sure?"

"I believe so. But don't—"

"I wouldn't think of it," Jessie agreed.

The hotel was divided off into dozens of rooms and a maze of corridors by means of flimsy portable partitions. Each room was furnished with a cheap iron cot with one blanket and no conveniences other than a packinghouse dresser, a pitcher of water, and a tallow candle.

"And I complained about the El Centro being bad," Ki growled, after they had locked their bags in their respective rooms.

A fifty-by-hundred-foot dining-and barroom adjoined the lobby. There Jessie and Ki breakfasted on fried potatoes, steak, and coffee. An apple pie in a cheescloth case caught Ki's eye, and he finished on it. It was now eight A.M. Jessie had two men to see. One was Delivan, of course. The other operated the stage line, a man named Peck Adams. It being immaterial to her which she saw first, Jessie decided to see whether stage men rose as early as railroad men.

When they went out again, Lobos had awakened by a few more degrees. Through brisk sidewalk traffic they walked to the eastern edge of town. The crowds were in a hilarious mood, with much horseplay, jostling, good-natured chaff. Men talked largely of what they would do with the money that would soon be in their hands, keeping their eyes peeled eastward, where the twin steel ribbons of the railroad stretched into the distance until the parallel lines seemed to meet. At the end of the main street, Jessie and Ki came to the Adams Stage Lines depot, which consisted of a large corral and a small adobe building with a porte-cochere at the side. Just as they were entering, men in the street began shouting and pointing. Far to the east, a shadow-blurred black object had appeared, crowned by a dark and wavering plume.

"Here comes our dough!" a brawny tracklayer yelled. "Get ready, boys!"

The waiting room of the depot was empty. Jessie rapped on the counter. A back door opened, and a large, unshaven man in trousers, underwear, and no shirt came out. He wore his hair far down his neck, though he was nearly bald, and his arms were massive. Thumbing a suspender strap over his shoulder, he glanced at Jessie and then Ki, and then back at her. "Wish for something, ma'am?" he asked.

"I'm looking for Peck Adams. If I'm early—"

"Come on back," the man said. "I'm Adams. Will you have a bait of breakfast?"

"I'd admire some coffee," Jessie said easily.

It was a middle-aged, futile-looking room, Jessie thought. In the corners, a bachelor's broom had seen, heard, and disclosed no evil. The rug resembled a very old toupee; an iron cookstove beside the sink was crusted with grease and rust. The bed had not been made, and probably would not be. An old mahogany commode beside an outer door bulged with boots and clothing.

Adams pulled on a shirt and then slid a skillet from the oven. "I could throw in some more side-pork as easy as not."

Studying the hefty man in the spotted calico shirt and brown trousers, Jessie looked quickly for the key to him and decided it was casualness: Don't hurry a man like Adams or he'd turn mulish. He commenced amputating fat rashers of bacon, and Jessie said, "Thanks, we've eaten."

"Staying at a hotel?"

"The Belle."

"Used to stay there m'self, until I got runnin' into railroad men every day. Maybe I'm choosy. I started bachin'."

Ki raised the lid of a blue enamel coffeepot. It was deep with ancient grounds. He started to throw them out, but Adams said, "Whoops! Whoops!" and took the pot from him. "That's the mother," he explained. He added six tablespoons of coarsely ground coffee and handed it back, smiling. "That's the mother. Orphan coffee ain't worth swillin'."

Ki chuckled; adding water, he placed the pot on the stove. "This is a friendly town," he observed. "Visitors get asked to breakfast before you know it."

"Food's cheap," Adams replied.

While the room filled with the woody smoke of bacon, the stage man set a small table of splintery deal. Suddenly the room began to vibrate, and a low growl seemed to rise from the floor. Glancing out a side window, they could see the distant train grow and take shape, slanting rays from the morning sun glancing off its stack and cowcatcher. A spurt of smoke soared over the boiler of the locomotive, a 4-4-0 Cooke, whose simple wheel arrangement allowed it to negotiate the sharpest curves. Adams yanked out a stick that had supported a pane of the double-hung window. The window crashed down but continued to rattle.

"Goddamn brimstone-burnin' junk heaps!" he said angrily.

"It's runnin' on a well-ballasted road," Jessie said as the trembling increased. "In another year you'll be able to shave in here and not cut yourself."

"Another year of this, ma'am, and I'll be doin' my damndest to cut my throat." He set the table and poured mugs of coffee, handing one to Jessie and another to Ki. "Too strong for you?"

"I only drink for the effect," Jessie said. She stirred sandy gray sugar into the coffee and watched Adams eat. "Don't think much of railroads, do you?"

"Ma'am," Adams said, "I used to think there was nothing meaner ner dirtier than a drunken Apache. Shows you how wrong a man can be."

"And now you're right on the point of having a railroad to compete with. Going to lick it?"

"I count on the horse sense of the good people of California to keep me in business," Adams declared. "Who'd pay money to have cinders blowed in his eyes, sparks in his hair, and be cremated in live steam every time the damn thing jumps the tracks, when he could ride a stage?"

"Spoken like a staging man," Jessie said. "Will you tell me something else? Why do you allow the M&SD to build the road, when you've got a charter that guarantees you exclusive franchise in this area? You could slap the railroad with an injunction and shut it down."

Adams drank coffee, investigated with his tongue the hiding places of food about his gums, and then asked cagily, "How'd you know about that?"

"I spend time checking out companies that I might invest in," Jessie said candidly, smiling into the man's frosty gray eyes. "You see, I'm thinking of buying a piece of your stage company."

"Oh, you are, are you?" Adams wiped his mouth on his cuff. "Now *you* tell *me* something. Why is everybody in Lobos in such a hell-sweat to invest in a line that's about to be drove to the wall?"

"I didn't know they were."

"You don't know about this other young woman? This widow woman? Ballard, I think she calls herself?"

"No. My money is Starbuck money. I'm Jessica Starbuck, and this's my friend, Ki, and—"

"Starbuck! But you're buildin' the M&SD! You're in railroadin'!"

"It's true I'm backing the M&SD, but I'm not limited to railroads. I'm in transportation, and I believe a stage and freight outfit can work hand-in-glove with a railroad. A railroad is more profitable on long hauls, but companies like yours are better at short hauling."

"If you think I'd sell out to you or—"

"Not at all. I'm thinking of buying in as a junior partner, investing in new equipment and expanded service, and letting you run your show as you see fit. Ballard," Jessie reflected. "Where's she from?"

"The Coast. Her late husband was with Rover Lines. Fine man, Rover."

"How old is she?"

"Your age. Almost as pretty."

"What does Rover have to say about her?"

"What does . . . ? Oh, you mean have I checked her out? No, no need to, Miz Starbuck. Take my word, Mrs. Ballard is as innercent as a babe. She was brought up in stagin', and wants to stay with it."

"Have you given her a commitment?" Jessie locked her shouting anxiety behind a calm voice. She had a hunch that Mrs. Ballard was fronting for someone out to scuttle the railroad. All the widow would have to do was buy in as a fifty-one-percent partner, and Adams would wake up with someone else in control, who'd immediately exercise the franchise. Even an outlaw like Tornado Turnbeau, crude and direct as he was, would know the bait to use for a trap.

"She's made me an offer," Adams said. "A good price, but she wants control, also. And I ain't so green as to make a hoss-breaker out of myself."

Jessie finished her coffee and rose. "I'm talking cash, Mr. Adams. I'm no fly-by-nighter. I'm dead serious."

Adams pumped water into a teakettle. "And I'm serious about not selling over forty-nine percent, ma'am." He winked at Ki. "Don't try to beat my time with Rita Ballard, either."

Ki smiled at what he assumed was a joke.

They left the stage office just as the pay-car train was wheezing into town. The crowd whistled and whooped as the pounding engine unit and its bobtail haul of modified baggage car and a shorty caboose came trundling and swaying over the track that ran down the middle of the main street. Jessie and Ki shouldered their way through the crowd, heading back in the direction of the hotel, and came abreast of the Belle of Lobos just as the locomotive began chugging past them. The engineer leaned out and yelled something that pleased the crowd. Voices cheered, and the engineer pulled the whistle cord. The shrilling scream cut through the rumble of the voices like a knife.

The sound frightened the standing twenty-mule team parked in front of the hotel. Left to their own devices by the jug-toting whacker, the long team jackknifed, the leaders doubling back upon the string behind. And twenty drooping, hipshot mules suddenly were transformed into a single brown mass of kicking, biting, bellowing cussedness.

The gears on the lead wagon had jackknifed as the team doubled back, and the hickory reach snapped with a report like a cannon shot. The bleary-eyed mule hacker spun around as if he'd been shot at, caught sight of his own reflection in the boiler plate of the passing locomotive, and, roaring in rage and fright, emptied his pistol at his own inebriate image. Then he wheeled again and ran bawling to his team.

He found the saddle wheeler, all right. But, blind drunk, he did not notice that she was facing in the opposite direction. Stumbling up to her from the Indian side, he grabbed a stirrup and swung himself up to straddle the hornless army saddle, facing the animal's clipped, nervous tail. For an instant he peered nearsightedly at the place where the mule's head should have been, his drunken features tense with awe. Then anger set his face to working.

"Shit! They done shot my wheeler's head clean off!" he bellowed. "C'mon out, you sneaks, and fight me fair!"

At that moment, the parted reach released the wagon's front wheels from beneath the three-ton load, and the bed struck the ground with an earth-shaking jar. The liquored skinner gasped and fell sideways from the saddle, and lay kicking in the dust.

Ki saw trouble developing, and he knew the behavior tendencies of government mules. Roaring a command, he started toward the melee. The team leaders were well-trained mules, up to a point. At the sound of that authoritative voice, they broke from the brawling mass and lined out, dragging the swing team after them. The whole string had straightened out in disorderly fashion long before Ki reached them, but with mulish afterthought, they had headed in the wrong direction. Squealing yet, kicking at the chain that barked their hocks, and unrestrained by load or line, the string headed for Ki, swinging the massive wagon gears behind like a wicked scythe.

The crowd fled widely, breaking over Ki like an avalanche, bearing him backward. It was like swimming against a raging current that carried him back in spite of himself. A rushing, heavily muscled grader struck him with his shoulder, almost knocking him off his feet. And, once on his back in that charging human herd, he would have been trampled. Angered, Ki grabbed the workman by the scruff of the neck, steadied himself with the other's weight, and drove the palm of his hand into the whiskered face. The grader grunted and staggered back, colliding with the pushing throng behind. Someone cursed and struck him from behind. The grader wheeled away, giving Ki a wide berth.

The crowd surged toward Ki once more. But the grader had provided a temporary breakwater against the flood, and Ki now had both feet squarely on the ground. A gambler came at him, panic etched on his white face. Ki smashed him in the face, adding a red pattern to the white. The gambler gave ground. Ki struck a pack-laden peddler who pressed behind the gambler. The peddler dropped his pack and followed the gambler.

The crowd parted around Ki as water breaks around a jagged rock, sweeping past him, the team bearing down behind them. At a hardware store next to the hotel, the runaway mules careened, just as the shopkeeper appeared in the open doorway to see what was going on. The keeper halted in the doorway, blinking at the nightmare of wall-eyed mules that stampeded past him, so close he could have reached out a hand and lost it to the long white teeth that flashed before his eyes. Then the nightmare passed, and he saw the heavy wagon gears swinging at him through the air, the massive wheels a full foot off the ground. With a wavering cry of hapless complaint, he fell backward from sight. A split second later the gears struck the storefront a shattering blow. There was a prolonged crash and the entire wooden structure disintegrated as if a bomb had exploded beneath it. The wheeler's doubletrees snapped under the stress of the impact, and the wagon gears remained in the ruins of the store.

The mules came on, tripping over the trailing chain. Ki waited, crouching, until the wheel team was abreast of him. With one hand, he grabbed up the single trailing line. With the other, he grabbed a handful of harness as the saddle mule flashed past. The excruciating jerk almost pulled his arm from his shoulder socket. But he held on. And the force of the violent haul catapulted him up astride of the saddle mule's back.

Another twenty seconds would have closed the gap between the runaway team and the fleeing crowd—and the slaughter would have been appalling. But, bracing himself in the kidney-pad saddle, Ki dragged at the jerkline, hand over hand, turning the leaders back. Then, not content with changing the direction of their stampede, he continued to haul at the long hemp line that connected with the bridle of the near lead mule, winding the entire mule string up in a compact milling knot.

For a moment the bellowing and biting and kicking continued, and Ki feared that the fire-eyed fiends would disembowel one another in that confused fray. But he kept them milling from the driver's seat and talked mule talk to them—caustic and threatening and adequately profane. Chastened and reassured by that familiar authoritative sound, the long-eared culprits gradually acknowledged their master and accepted defeat. The bellowing and the striking ceased, and the milling became more orderly. At length, the milling ceased, and the mules stood still, sides heaving and mouths frothing.

They were still wild-eyed and edgy. But Ki astride the wheeler told them of the fate awaiting those who disturbed the peace again, and they took his word for it. A couple of stablehands from the livery arrived to take over, and they inquired respectfully of Ki what should be done with the mules.

Thinking of the livery hostler's outrageous rates, Ki answered, "Lock 'em up on bread and water for sixty days and nights!" Then under Ki's nitric eye came the drunken whacker, who was stirring in the dust where he had fallen. Sliding down from the postage-stamp saddle, Ki added, "Better stable that one with the mules." Then he left the mules and the sweating hands on their own and started back to Jessie.

Shouldering his way through the returning crowd, he was about halfway back to Jessie when he noticed a girl heading determinedly toward him. Her blue eyes met his in a frank, long look that telegraphed a challenge and an invitation that Ki was not inclined to ignore. Then he caught on that she was not intent so much on him as on a woman's trampled handbag lying close-by. He picked it up and was surprised to feel its weight. He wiped the dust from it and saw that it was made of thick cowhide, elaborately tooled by experienced craftsmen. He didn't need to look twice at the heavy clasp and massive strap to see that they were high-carat gold, the strap finely engraved with the initials R. A. H.

The young woman had pushed through to him now. Ki looked up from the handbag just as her step lagged, and in the next moment she stumbled over a stone in the uneven street bed. He heard her gasp as he reached to catch her by the waist. He experienced a soft and fragrant collision, but an instant later she was pulling away. If nothing else, he knew her waist was not boned to such slenderness.

Her blue eyes still held challenge and invitation. There was admiration, too. And something else which he could not quite fathom. "You were wonderful!" the blue eyes exclaimed, in a voice that was husky and theatrical. "You saved a lot of lives. Even mine, perhaps. And you've found my bag."

Ki grinned, handing her the bag. "My pleasure, Miss . . . ?"

"Mrs. Ballard."

"Mrs. *Rita* Ballard?"

She gripped her bag with tense fingers. "Do we . . . we know each other, sir?"

Ki made a slight bow. "My name is Ki, Mrs. Ballard. You were described to me and my friend, Miss Starbuck."

"By whom?" She tried to smile; her lip trembled.

"By a mutual aquaintance."

"Our mutual aquaintance failed to describe you, Mr. . . . Ki."

"Just Ki. We're in transportation."

Rita Ballard was utterly off-balance, and Ki was boldly inspecting her. Her hair, uncovered by a bonnet, had been encouraged to glistening darkness by a brush; her face was snub-nosed, freckled, and lush-lipped. She was petite and deep-bosomed, nary a straight line in her body.

All at once she moved to pass him, raising her skirt with one hand. "Good morning, Mis—er, Ki. You have the wrong Mrs. Ballard."

He stood aside, watching her sashay off. "And you, Mrs. Ballard, have the wrong name," he said gravely. "Or the wrong bag, with the initials R. A. H."

★

Chapter 4

At the western edge of town the railroad yard was clamorous with activity. With a clanging of brake rigging, a screeching from the rising safety valve, and a banging of couplers, the pay train ground to a halt on the sidetrack closest to the depot. Armed guards descended from the caboose and took up posts alongside both sides of the baggage car. The pay doors opened; the brass-grilled windows banged up. A steady stream of men began filing in one door and out the other. Payday at Lobos was a reality.

Other laborers were on the job. Chuffing work engines were shunting supplies for delivery to rail end, and the roundhouse sheds reverberated with the clang of heavy repairs. Yet the yard itself was relatively small, and Jessie and Ki had little difficulty in locating Otis Delivan's office—a personal day coach on a sidetrack near the stubby new depot.

Lights glowed in the coach, and posted by the steps at both ends were placards reading PRIVATE. Ignoring the notices, Jessie and Ki climbed to the iron-railed front platform and rapped on the door. After a short delay it was opened by a squat, ferret-eyed man wearing dark trousers and a sleeve-gartered shirt.

"Mr. Delivan, please," Jessie said.

"No, Mr. Delivan is busy." The man started closing the door. "You'll have to have an appointment. Come back tomorrow."

"We're expected," Jessie countered testily, wedging her foot in the doorway. "Tell Mr. Delivan that Miss Starbuck has arrived."

"Oh, dear," the man said, paling. He relinquished his hold on the door and gestured for them to enter. "I didn't know, I . . . Wait here, please."

"Here" proved to be the forward compartment of the austerely appointed coach. The man went through a connecting door, and a moment later he returned, accompanied by an imposingly tall and broad-shouldered man.

"Ah, Miss Starbuck! And Ki! So good to see you again," the big man said in greeting, his movements quick and decisive as he approached and shook hands in a warm grip. His eyes held only friendliness, but the first man's were narrowed warily. The large man chuckled. "You'll have to excuse Emil, I'm afraid. Like every good aide, he doesn't trust anybody. At times I believe he's even suspicious of me."

"I can't understand how, Mr. Delivan."

"Otis, I insist. No sense in standing on stuffy formalities in such a gawdforsaken spot as Lobos," Delivan replied genially, escorting her and Ki through the connecting door. He shut the door, leaving Emil looking irritated in the forward compartment, and turned to another man who was standing expectantly in the rear section of the coach. "Miss Starbuck, Ki, I'd like you to meet Vernon Hodge, owner of the Arcadia Survey and Development Company, out of Calexico."

During introductions, Jessie sized up Vernon Hodge. A middling-size, middling-aged man, he had a swarthy face with a prominent, high-bridged nose, a hard mouth, and conspicuous cheekbones. He was immaculately dressed and barbered, his hair dark brown and styled with short sideburns that blended into a mustache and full General Grant beard.

In comparison, Otis Delivan had unruly red hair that emphasized the metallic grayness of his widely spaced eyes—eyes whose pupils had shrunk to pinpoints of black from long looking into the vast luminous distances of the Southwest. His hands were the hands of a gambler, or a gunman, but his weathered face and muscular shoulders hinted of more vigorous pursuits. His somber, custom-made clothes fitted him well, yet he looked uncomfortable and out of place in such civilian attire.

Jessie was impressed. If she were forced to choose between Delivan and the exquisite Hodge, she knew she'd pick Delivan, wrinkles and all. He was not only a man's man, but a woman's man as well.

The rear compartment appeared to be Delivan's office on wheels and living quarters when he was away from the hotel, with a bunk and a washstand along one side, and a flat table, a set of filing cabinets, and some hardback chairs along the other. The table was a compost heap of charts and relief maps, which, evidently, Delivan and Hodge had been consulting when Jessie and Ki arrived.

"Miss Starbuck," Hodge said, smiling, "I've been

warned about you. Toughest entrepreneur in the West." He spoke as though it were a compliment. "And from what I've heard you are not the person to regret any action which slows up the progress of the M&SD."

"Legal action," Jessie admitted, "in accordance with the laws of the land."

"I presume you're aware of Mr. Delivan's plans to run the track through the Lagunas and over Espina Pass in the Cuyamacas?"

"I am. And I've every confidence he'll succeed."

"Over the mountains," Delivan said stoutly, "or under 'em. We'll get across." He paused, then went on. "I've given Miss Starbuck my figures on the cost, Vernon. It'll run high per mile when we hit the mountains, but we intend to build."

Vernon Hodge nodded grimly. "You've seen the Cuyamacas in the summer," he pointed out. "They're a lot different with six feet of snow in the pass. The figures you've given Miss Starbuck might well be doubled." He turned to Jessie and made a sweeping gesture at the maps. "To turn south and skirt the hills along the border would be greatly cheaper."

"Vern," Delivan responded, before Jessie could speak, "I realize that you control a lot of land down thataway that you'd love to unload on settlers, but I ain't buildin' this railroad for your benefit. By going over, or through, the Cuyamacas, we'll save more'n two hundred haulage miles. Think what that'll mean when we really begin hauling freight. We'll have the shortest, straightest link 'twixt Mexico, the Southern Pacific transcontinental line, and coastal ports."

"Well, take my word for this, Otis," Hodge replied flatly. "Despite your ability and Miss Starbuck's backing, the M&SD will never reach the Cuyamacas Mountains by this winter, let alone go through them." He turned on his heel and, with a parting nod to Jessie and Ki, strode out of the compartment.

Somewhat startled by Hodge's sharp, abrupt behavior, Jessie cast a quizzical look at Delivan. "Was he threatening us?"

"No, I'm sure not. Vernon argues and wheedles to get me to change the route southward so he can clean up in land speculatin'—and gets mad and calls me boneheaded contrary when I refuse—but he don't need to voice threats. He's just airin' what everybody else likes to advise me, about losin' out not only to the mountains but to Tornado Turnbeau and his cutthroat crew as well."

"Hasn't the sheriff been able to run Turnbeau down?"

"Sheriffs. And marshals, posses, vigilantes, and every other stripe of lawdog operation. Nope, they all been riding in circles and gettin' nowhere. Turnbeau just keeps on raiding the railroad, slayin' my men in cold blood, in between his reg'lar occupations like smugglin', stage robbin', and rustlin'. Tornado Turnbeau is a thoroughly unprincipled person and, in my opinion, the receptacle of all vices." Delivan paused, picking up a black briar pipe and tamping in blacker tobacco. "Well, all vices 'cept one—moonshinin'. That one's won hands down by White Water Whittaker. He's also been accused, but never convicted, of horse stealin' and beef butcherin', along with peddling whiskey to breeds and Indians."

Listening to Delivan, Jessie watched through the coach windows as a supply train approached nearby. For a moment Delivan stopped talking, unable to be heard as the train's exhaust deepened and swelled, its low rumble becoming a grinding roar. Abruptly the exhaust was closed off and the couplers clanked together as the train quickly lost speed, nearing the new roundhouse. The switch to a siding flashed red, the engineer slackened speed still more, and the slowing locomotive nosed onto the chosen track, in the shadow of the roundhouse wall. Jessie could make out the engineer leaning from the cab, one hand on the brake handle. The fireman stood in the gangway between engine and tender, gazing out at the town. As the noise dissipated, Jessie turned back to Delivan and asked, "Any luck negotiating crossing rights with Whittaker?"

"Jessie, you should've seen the lawyer I sent out to see Whittaker at his Blister River digs. I must admit Pettifog is a mite pompous, deckin' out as he does in white vest and choker collar and red tie, but that ain't no call for Whittaker to call him a pinched-beaked shyster, and to send him packin' back here in just his long johns, tied across his saddle by his own galluses." Delivan struck a match, puffed a few times, and continued. "At least me 'n' Peck Adams are talking. Not getting nowhere, but we're talking. I've yet to understand why he don't just slap us with an injunction and stop construction on the line. And as for gaining the right-of-way over Espina Pass . . . Well, I have to admit I'm glad to see you, Jessie. P'raps with all the resources of the Starbuck organization on the lookout, we'll be able to locate the heirs of Don Fundador and negotiate rights across them grant lands in time to—"

The rest of his words was lost in a deafening explosion. Without the slightest warning, a cloud of yellow smoke was gushing from under the work train's locomotive; there was a rending of metal and a rumble of cascading bricks. Through the turmoil knifed a scream of agony, cut off short.

Through the billowing smoke cloud, Jessie, Ki, and Delivan, half-stunned by the shock of the explosion, saw the locomotive actually rise in the air. It careened off the tracks and turned over. An instant later there was a second thundering roar as the boiler exploded. Huge chunks of steel whizzed through the air. A small building near the tracks was torn to pieces by a section of the hurtling boiler. More bricks flew wildly from the shattered roundhouse. A cloud of steam streaked through the smoke, and for an instant all details of the catastrophe were blotted out.

Already Delivan, with Jessie and Ki at his heels, was dashing from his coach. By the time they reached the outside, the smoke and steam were dissipating, and they could see that where the tracks had been a moment before was a wide and deep crater, still wisping smoke. One whole side of the roundhouse had been torn away. The roof sagged crazily on is splintered beams. The turntable had been blown from its pivot and lay, smashed and twisted, in the pit. Of the fireman and engineer nothing was to be seen.

The depot and train yard were a turmoil of near panic. From behind, crowds were boiling from the saloons and eateries, shouting, gesturing, thronging in and milling around the scene, to stare awed at the crater, bawl angry questions, and curse for lack of answers.

Jessie, Ki, and Otis Delivan, his eyes like burning

coals, sprinted away from the coach and shouldered their way to the front. A score of paces distant from the track, they spotted a portion of the mangled engineer. The fireman was apparently nothing but scattered fragments. Parts of the locomotive were strewn in every direction, along with splintered cross-ties and twisted rails.

Plowing through the crowd loomed a bulky figure. Another moment and a barrel-chested man with gray-streaked hair and a salt-and-pepper handlebar mustache was frowning down at the crater, his sagging vest pinned with a silver badge marked Sheriff. "Sounded like a bomb," the lawman declared irately. "Black-powder bomb, I'd bet on it. Some skunk planted it under the tracks and set it off when the train came."

"Zeigler, that's hard to believe!" Delivan protested, although with his own eyes he was forced to believe. "The track is patrolled, and we have our own security. Only way would be if one of our own construction workers was a double-crosser. But I trust them all!"

"Well, there's the evidence," Sheriff Zeigler said grimly, making a sweeping gesture while glancing around. Catching sight of Jessie, and apparently figuring a female wouldn't lie, he asked her, "Ma'am, were you witness to this?"

Jessie nodded and introduced herself and Ki. "Yes, we were with Mr. Delivan in his coach and saw it through the window. I'm afraid a charge went off under the engine, just like a bomb."

"Believe me, I'll find out how it got there," Delivan vowed grimly. Then, with a light pressure of fingers on Jessie's arm, he turned her so he could speak confidentially, out of earshot of the sheriff and others. "This is presumptuous of me, being short notice and all, but I think we should get together to talk soon."

"Of course, anytime."

"For dinner, in my coach at seven-thirty?"

"Fine."

"My pleasure. Until then, unfortunately, I'll have this to contend with." Delivan turned back, saying in a louder voice, "Thank God, Sheriff, this isn't worse. If this had been one of our trains loaded with workers this morning, instead of a freight . . ."

Delivan and the sheriff began ramrodding the sometimes grisly tasks that needed to be done. What could be found of the dead fireman and engineer had to be located and carried away, and the rubble had to be searched. A gang was hastily gotten together to repair the disrupted tracks. The workers moved cautiously, handling their picks and shovels gingerly, as if fearing that other bombs might be planted about.

The tragedy cast a pall on the payday spree. As the crowd dispersed from the train yard, some regrouped tensely in the street, while others headed back to their jobs. Most went to various saloons in tense groups, to discuss over drinks this latest outrage, their exhilaration and excitement of the morning dead as ditch water.

After the crowd had dispersed, Jessie and Ki still lingered at the scene of the explosion. They examined the fragments of the wrecked engine and estimated the depth and size of the crater the black powder had hollowed out. They were particularily interested in the twisted rails and the splintered cross-ties scattered about. Finally they located a ponderous oaken tie, or rather, half of one, some distance from the right-of-way.

"This is the one the charge was under, all right," Jessie decided. "Half of it is blown away and there're powder burns on the end here."

"But how was it done?" Ki asked.

Shaking her head, Jessie started toward the hotel.

Ki stuck around a while longer, going over the area with the utmost care, until he had satisfied himself that there were no hidden wires that led to an electric detonator concealed somewhere. No, the charge had not been fired from a distance. But how in hell was it done?

Frowning, glancing about perplexed, Ki caught sight of the young woman named Rita Ballard approaching, stepping daintily across the rubble. He waited, curious, for her to reach him, his expression flat, blank.

"Horrid," she said, coming up to him. "Simply horrid."

"Did you see it happen?"

"No, but I certainly heard it."

"Uh-huh. Well, what brings you here now?"

Rita looked down at her feet, then up at Ki. "After we met this morning, I discovered that we really do have something in common."

"Really?"

"We're both interested in buying into Mr. Adams's line."

"I'm not personally. Miss Starbuck is. Why are you?"

"My husband was in staging. He died two years ago."

"You married young," Ki observed.

"I suppose."

"What did your husband die of?" Ki's smile was a softness at the corners of his mouth. He watched her intently.

"They . . . they didn't . . ." She touched the bosom of her dress. "Pneumonia, they thought."

"A pity." Ki sighed. "Hard to adjust, I know. Birthdays recall the departed . . . anniversaries. When was your anniversary, by the way?"

"The . . . the Fourth of July, I think," she said softly.

"Not sure?"

She pressed her lips together. "What are you trying to find out? What business is this of yours?"

"What you're trying to do. Wreck Adams, the railroad, or both."

Her eyes sparked. "I consider that a crude and—"

"I consider spying crude," Ki said. "You're trying to get control of his stage line for someone else, someone who wants to use his franchise to stop the railroad. Isn't that the whole deal in a nutshell?"

Her mouth was drab with fury or shock. Fire glinted in her eyes. "Except for making an embarrassing scene in public," she snapped, "I should slap you. We have nothing else to say to each other." Pivoting on her heel, she stalked off in a snit.

"Except," Ki said as he eyed her departing form, "that it's too bad. There ought to be a law against girls so pretty going into spying. Poor ol' Peck Adams. He's being taken, hook, line, and sinker."

As the western hills changed from hard gray to misty cobalt, and the staring eyes of the windows became squares and rectangles of gold, the town regained something of the hilarity of the morning. Right up to evening, spikers and graders and tie cutters, cooks and rail layers and trestlemen—the vast legion of brawny laborers who were cogs in the mighty machinery of the railroad building—had passed in line through the paycar, drawing their wages. Now the money was finding its way across bar counters, into dance-hall tills, into the pockets of gamblers by way of faro and poker and chuck-a-luck.

While the blue dusk was sifting down from the hills, Jessie left the hotel and crossed through the train yard to Otis Delivan's coach. Crews were still working, she saw, repairing damaged track and clearing away debris, and one group was just finishing placement of the turntable. The shattered roundhouse appeared to need at least one more day to have its roof shored up.

Delivan's aide, Emil, greeted Jessie more pleasantly than he had before. This time he was clad in a steward's white mess jacket. The coach had been cleaned in her honor, the major miracles having been accomplished in the rear section. The chart table was covered with linen and arranged for two. Coffee-mug vases held sprays of wildflowers, and Otis Delivan appeared in an unwrinkled shirt and neat tie.

"Jessie, you're a pip late, just socially perfect," he greeted cheerily. "You look ravishing, far superior to the dinner, I'm afraid."

Dinner was a catered affair, Emil serving it from the crew mess tent nearby. The food was standard employee fare, meaning it was healthy, plentiful, and often bland—yet rules were that it was fine enough for worker and manager alike. Booze was a perquisite of management, though, and Delivan had some wines stashed for just such occasions as this.

Dinner flowed well. Jessie found herself confirming her impressions of Delivan as a shrewd, self-made man, not rich by current standards, but confident enough to hold opinions without being opinionated. True, he was in his early forties, but his type were just hitting their prime then, and she felt his age an attraction.

There was no question that he found her an attraction. Delivan was all business, yet he had sufficiently broad interest that he could appreciate her two-piece outfit of powder-blue Venetian wool, and could recognize it as a creation both stylish and fashionable—two discouraging words rarely heard in Lobos.

Afterward they helped Emil tidy up. Delivan unearthed a half bottle of brandy, and Emil asked if he'd care for glasses on the deck. Jessie perked up, asking, "A platform deck?"

"Yes, but no chairs. I sleep there on hot nights."

"Is your cot or bed or whatever fit to be seen?"

"Aye, she's a proper mattress, and proper clad, too."

Jessie gave a laugh. "Then let's pay her a call."

Bottle in hand, with Emil trailing behind, Delivan ushered Jessie out the rear door. The observation deck was longer than a regular coach vestibule. It was bounded on its three open sides by a waist-high brass rail, and was carpeted with a thick horsehair mattress that was covered in turn with blankets and a navy bedspread.

"Hotel bunks cramp me," Delivan said. "This's nice and big."

"Big doesn't always mean respectable," Jessie quipped.

"At what she cost me to be special-made, believe me, she's respectable." He poured brandies, and as Emil went back in, he gave Jessie a snifter, then toasted and sipped. "Now, where were we? Oh yes, you were telling me about this mysterious Jimenez Linares and the Cantina Cara Dura."

"Well, I've pretty well told you all I know, with the half a coin and everything. But to me, the real mystery is Linares stabling our horses here in Lobos, and then, apparently, not taking another mount to travel on."

"P'raps he has a friend here with horses. Or his own."

"Maybe," Jessie said with a shrug. "Or maybe it means he's around town somewhere. In any case, I'm in no hurry to chase after him right now."

"I'll put out the word to look for him," Delivan said, and excused himself to go speak to Emil. Jessie didn't mind being left alone on the deck, but settled comfortably with her brandy and gazed afar at the burnished gray buttes . . . and lower, at the dusky, lamp-glowing main street . . . and nearer, at the broken wall of the roundhouse, where she could glimpse workmen hoisting the boiler off a damaged locomotive. And that was how Delivan found her when he came back, sitting on the mattress, relaxing dreamily.

"Don't say you're sorry," she said. "I'm not."

He sat down beside her. "Okay, I'll just say the coach will jolt in a few minutes. It'll be hooking onto a short freight that's deadheading to rail end. Why don't you come along with me? It's a splendid ride at night.

"Don't tempt me. But there's no place for me to sleep."

Delivan mulled that one over. "Hmm," he said, and was still thinking when the coach lurched and swayed. Ahead of the coach was the backing freight, the couplers thundering together and drawbars grating metallically as the engine hammered the train's tail car against the coach's front.

Sent almost sprawling, Delivan regained his balance and tried to reassure Jessie. "It won't bother us. It's not leaving for a while."

She rose anyway. "I believe I'd better say good night."

"P'raps. I've nothing left to offer after this," he said ruefully, standing with the almost empty bottle. "Let's kill it."

Jessie smiled. "All right, I'll split one last drink."

While he carefully measured the brandy into their snifters, Delivan sighed and said, "Probably just as well you don't ride along, Jessie. The crews are scared to move without first inspecting everything, and it's about all the foremen can do to keep 'em picking and poking. They're nervous, edgy." Moodily, Delivan stared down at his drink, swirling it slow and easy as he spoke. "Another bomb like today's, and they're liable to go on general strike."

Jessie looked at him over the rim of her glass. "We might be able to prevent another one, if we could figure out how this one was set off. Ki and I looked around the site and found the oak tie that the charge was under. It seems to us that the bomber must've used some kind of timing apparatus, but how did he set it to explode the charge right at the time that train was passing over that spot?"

"You've got a puzzler there, okay. A dozen trains passed thisaway since morning, and it's sure the stuff wasn't planted after daylight. That supply train wasn't running on any schedule, and even if it had been, the timing would've had to be split-second. Any sign of hidden wires leadin' to a detonator?"

"No, Ki double-checked for that. The charge had not been fired from a distance. That's what makes us think of a timing device. That the timing had been set by pure coincidence for the exact moment the train would hit that spot seems ridiculous. There's the remote possibility, of course, that the charge was fired by the shock of the passing train, but if this was so, why hadn't it been exploded by one of the other trains that went by earlier?"

Delivan didn't respond at once, but moved to lean against the deck rail, where he eyed the yard beyond. "Sheriff Zeigler's right. It must be sabotage, the work of one of my own men against me. I wonder who—"

The coach shuddered, clanking, a reminder that it was due to depart. Jessie said, "I think I'd better go."

"I reckon." He drained his brandy, then reached across and grasped Jessie's left hand in his. "What's the etiquette on this?"

They stood that way for a few moments. Jessie wasn't thinking of social rules, but of how she'd grown to like him increasingly over the evening. She slid her hand free.

"Otis, I really must go," she insisted.

"Absolutely. And the rule, as I recall, is that I'm to see you off."

"Please do, if it says it's at my pleasure, not your leisure. Well? Are you escorting me up front, or tossing me over back here?"

"Whichever you prefer," he answered affably. "Whichever, I'd prefer to say good night here. I won't have a chance once I toss you out, and Emil might be still lurking up front."

"Fine, first we say good night, then I leave."

"Good night, Jessie."

"Good night."

He bent over as though to give a chaste good-night peck. And she raised her chin to offer her lips for the same. But the kiss that developed was anything but a chaste peck. Her mouth opened willingly beneath his, to the surprise of both of them. Delivan encircled her waist with his hands and tugged her closer to him. Tentatively her arms began to work their way around him, and then their bodies were rubbing against each other while their mouths worked together avidly.

Suddenly the coach jerked their feet out from under them. They landed in a tangle, the coach still shaking a little, their kiss broken and leaving them breathless. Jessie squirmed about to a sitting position and looked at Delivan as if it were all his fault.

"Otis, don't you dare say our powerful kissing knocked us down. I've been on trains enough to know slack being pulled."

"You read my mind. I swear the kisses did it."

"This is silly. What am I doing still on this train?"

"P'raps this will tell you," Delivan replied, and he kissed her again, his hand under her chin, pressing her mouth to his.

Jessie was startled to find herself kissing him again, but she was even more astounded by the subtle kick of it. It wasn't demanding or pressuring, nor carnal and lusty. It was warm and very sweet, and it touched something in her that made her feel very good about being kissed by Otis Delivan. And it felt very natural when he enclosed her in his arms again, their knees touching, their position awkward and tiring. But his lips were on hers, and she felt very sensual and yet very protected by his strong yet gentle yearning.

She began to feel vibrations then, and realized the train was starting slowly, slowly to move. The train, she sensed, was going a bit faster, and she really must stop this and she would in a second, after she touched the tip of his tongue with hers. It was a hot, sweet touch that made her melt inside.

Jessie then broke the kiss, but remained close enough to feel his hard breathing against her cheek. She whispered, "Otis, let me off this train at once. You are abducting me."

"I'd let you off in an instant, but we're moving too fast."

Turning, Jessie stared between the railing bars. They were gathering speed, she could see that, and were passing the dark bulk of the water tower and clattering over the main-line switch points. Nobody to cry for help to . . . even if she'd wanted to.

"I'll have you flogged, Otis, for kidnapping."

"Positively. And probably an extra dose of the lash for dragging you off by your hair, screaming and kicking. But first . . ."

Tenderly he pushed Jessie down on the platform mattress, then lay beside her, perched on his elbow.

He put his lips on hers softly, searchingly, and ran his tongue over her lips and pushed into her mouth to find rich heat. Jessie wriggled, sighing, squirming into a more comfortable position, settling herself down to luxuriate in his caress.

There was no more talking for a long while. Delivan was gentle, treating her as if she were very fragile, very dear. He moved close to her, putting the weight of his chest on her, placing his hands under her shoulders, and kissing her deeply. She started moaning and quivering, squirming as his fingers molded her sensitive breasts and found, under the tightness of her suit jacket and blouse, one of her nipples and teased it into vivid awareness . . . and they both knew it was time to remove all hindrances to their yearning bodies.

"I want to," he murmured, "like an onion."

Jessie smiled and lay back, enjoying the touch of his dexterous fingers. She leaned one way, then the other, raising her arms to help him remove her jacket. Then her blouse went, too, and Delivan smiled as he stared at her thrusting breasts and dark, jutting nipples. He gave each a kiss and moved on.

Kneeling, unfastening her skirt, Delivan pushed it over her arching pelvis and down her legs. Jessie helped kick it aside, leaving it with her shoes in a puddle on the mattress. She wasn't wearing a petticoat this time, there being only so much space in her small traveling case, but she had on a fine set of pantalets, made of Valenciennes lace and nearly translucent silk. Delivan had a bird's-eye view of the golden-red delta between her thighs as he untied the drawstring and eased her pantalets along her legs.

"Stunning, truly stunning," he murmured, and

bent forward to kiss her upper thigh, worming higher and more toward the inside. She gasped, stiffening in reflex, a shaft of pure delight shooting through her at his moist, open-mouthed touch. Nude, on a train's observation deck. Breasts firm, nipples painfully swollen. Legs open, forced open by this man's palms. He was doing exquisite things to her flesh, thrilling things that caused her to squrim with intense pleasure. Then, inevitably, he came to her.

Delivan tore off his clothing. Jessie eyed his bare form as appreciatively as he had studied hers. He was silhouetted in the softly moonlit sky, as the train continued chugging through the rolling countryside; and Jessie thought the naked man fit his surroundings well—a prime combination of strength and maturity. And virility, she noticed with something akin to trepidation.

And when he pressed between her parting legs, she watched the look on his face as he guided his thick, pulsating manhood forward. She opened herself wide, sprawling and spreading lasciviously, feeling his staff burrowing deep inside her moist furrow, throbbing, searching out every fold, every hidden nook and cranny. He paused then, lying upon her and pressing her breasts. She pushed up against him in return, and their eyes met, smiling, and he slowly began pumping.

"Yes," she sighed, eyes closing, "let's make steam . . ."

Delivan quickened his tempo with long, sawing strokes. There was only marginal yield to his mattress, and none to the hard flooring beneath. He kept on pounding her, and she kept demanding more, her yearning belly trying to swallow him whole. Her taut buttocks were buffeted against the mattress by his stormy hammerings. Straining hard, he plunged all the way into her wetly distended channel, gasping and panting with his surging urgency, his spiraling desire.

Jessie moaned beneath him, trying to match his insatiable beat. She listened to his hard breathing, then felt his hand sliding down between their bellies, lower and lower, until one finger was caressing her clitoris. The combination of the strokings was too much for her already emotion-torn senses. Her mouth filled his ears with inarticulate little cries. She could feel the swaying of the coach beneath her, as its steel wheels clacked over the rail joints in an ever-increasing tempo, in time to Delivan's ever more powerful thrusts.

"Ahhh, Lord!" Jessie wept, biting her lip, raking Delivan's back. The engine's whistle gave a long, shrill scream—or did it come from Jessie?—as she felt Delivan shudder, his warm eruption spewing far up inside her. Then her own inner muscles spasmed, tightening around his pulsating shaft.

They came together like a pair of colliding engines, and her passion exploded like a locomotive's boiler at full steam.

They might have been rolling through the flats near Lobos, but Jessie called it Paradise . . .

★

Chapter 5

Jessie was unprepared for the full impact of the dramatic scene awaiting her at end-of-track. Leaving Delivan's private coach at daybreak, she saw squads of workmen scurrying back and forth, unloading ties and rails from flatcars that had brought them up during the night. Smaller, horse-drawn cars rolled the rails, plates, and spikes up to the end of track, where the heavy ties were going down. A dozen men rushed at the car, grasped the rail and trotted forward with it, dropping it in place. Bolters nailed the rails down while the rail crew scrambled back for the next set of rails.

Delivan was already on the job, standing a short distance ahead of the rails, where men with picks and shovels were busy grading the right-of-way. Beyond, across the open flats, Jessie saw the dust raised by the scrapers and plows as the grading men filled in the hollows. Behind her, a switch engine was puffing busily, shunting cars from the main tracks onto a siding, sorting them out for convenient disposal. Nearer by, groups of men were following the rail bolters, spiking the rails permanently into place. Gandy dancers, foot on shovel shoulder, were tamping earth and stone under the newly placed ties, performing the eccentric shuffle with their feet that had given them their peculiar name. The heads of spike mauls flashed circles of light as the men drove the heavy spikes into the ties, clamping down the tie places and wedging the ponderous steel rails firmly into place. Foremen were busy with track gauges, making sure that the rails were uniformly spaced. Wrenchmen bolted the fishplates into place, securing the rails end to end with just the proper space between to take care of the expansion and contraction of the steel in hot or cold weather.

The switch engine came puffing back almost to where Jessie stood near the coach, pulling a single car loaded with cross-ties. It screeched to a halt as the engineer applied the air. Jessie saw him throw the reverse lever into forward position and reach for the throttle.

A switchman swung a target from white to red, opening the siding switch. He turned and energetically waved a "come-ahead" signal. A second switchman, standing on the front step of the locomotive, grasped the lever that would raise the coupling boom. The engine's drive wheels bit the rails, and turned over faster and faster. The switchman on the step sawed his hand up and down in the stop signal and jerked the lever, raising the pin and uncoupling the car from the engine. The engineer slammed his throttle shut and applied the air. The engine came to a quick halt, but the loaded car, reeling and rocking, took the switch points and whizzed down the siding.

"You kicked that one too damned hard!" the yard conductor bellowed irritably to the engineer. "Want to knock the drawbar out of it?"

There was a string of cars already on the siding. The car of ties struck the rearmost with a crash of coupling bars. The conductor opened his mouth to shout further profane protest—but what he said was never heard. It was drowned in a roaring explosion that seemed to cause even distant buttes to quake and reel.

Through a mushrooming cloud of yellowish smoke, Jessie could see splintered cross-ties, portions of the car and earth and stone flying in all directions. As the smoke cloud rose, thinning out, she could see that pieces of the car and its load of ties were scattered all over the area. The rails were twisted and broken. A hole in the ground showed where a car had stood. The engineer, dazed and bleeding, was picking himself up from the floor of his cab. One switchman lay unconscious; the other was running about crazily, as if bereft of his senses.

"I told you you kicked it too hard!" the yard conductor was insanely bawling, over and over again. "I told you you kicked it too hard!"

As Jessie's deafened ears resumed something approaching normal hearing, she realized that the pounding of the sledgehammers had ceased. The construction site rang with shouts and curses as the laborers began scrambling from the scene of the disaster. Delivan was running back this way as fast as he could, waving at the men, bawling for them to stand fast, trying to rally them. But with little success; it appeared that there wouldn't be much more work done today.

Jessie sprinted to the fallen switchman. An examination convinced her that the man was only stunned from the concussion, and had not been struck by flying debris. Turning him over to the engineer, who had a cut on his face but was otherwise unhurt, Jessie surveyed the scene. The crater was not as deep but was wider than the one hollowed out by the blast at the Lobos train yard yesterday. The tie-loaded car had been blown to fragments, its load scattered far and wide. The nearest two cars of the string ahead of it lay on their sides, their loads spilled on the ground. In general, however, the damage done was comparatively slight.

Delivan was almost to Jessie when suddenly, unexpectedly, a volley of rifle fire seared through the hazy smoke. Bullets ripped by, mere inches away, concentrating on her and Delivan.

"Get down!" she shouted to Delivan. "You're a prime target out here!" Then, to the workers milling nearby, she called, "Get cover! If you've got guns, grab them!" Taking her own advice, she plunged for concealment.

More guns were opening fire now. Except for a few workers short on brains, everyone dove in a chaotic rout for shelter behind boulders, machinery, stacks of supplies, or whatever was close.

Hugging the earth under a six-wheel wagon, Jessie searched for the source of the attack. Her first notion was the flanking hills alongside the tracks, but a bearded workman bellied up beside her and used his carbine to point toward the right-of-way.

"Gawd, it's like Injuns attacking!"

In a sense he was right, Jessie thought, but Indians weren't this rash. Eighteen, perhaps twenty, riders were streaming in to strike from the rear, wildly outnumbered by crewmen. They were figuring on surprise and on the workers still being shocked dimwitted—both of which, Jessie had to admit, were appallingly true. But she wondered if they were also counting on the workers being unarmed—which was mostly true, and those who had weapons might not have taken them to cover.

Delivan dove in on Jessie's other side, saying, "Not a spare gun to be found!" Then he winced, biting dirt, as a bullet nearly parted his hair.

The attackers split at the last moment into two curving waves that surged along the trackside lanes used by the wagons. Concentrating their lethal mayhem on the workers trapped in the middle, they poured in salvos, bullets riddling tools and equipment, and ricocheting off rubble left from construction.

The workman beside Jessie grunted, licked his thumb, and fired. He hit one rider in the breastbone and was tracking a second when he grunted and collapsed. Jessie glanced over and saw his suddenly sprouted third eye, and wormed his old, battered Winchester out of his grasp. Pressing her cheek against its stock, she lost no time in picking up where he'd left off, dropping another rider out of his saddle. She rolled, levering, to find a third.

Increasingly, the workers who had weapons were opening up, as the raiders swept farther along the sides. From the haphazard defense could be heard the throaty blasts of .50-90 Express rounds, and the sharper cracks of repeaters like Jessie's. Flanking them were pounding hooves and the drumming reports of .56-50 Spencer carbines, which the riders seemed to prefer. Some now could be spotted using glow-punks to ignite sticks of black powder, then hurling them with fuses sparking into the midst of the sheltering construction equipment.

It was a bold plan, Jessie realized in that instant. Destroy the machines and specialty tools, and the jobs were wiped out, even if the workers decided they wanted them. Assuming any workers would be alive to choose, after this blasting!

As fearfully aware as Jessie, the armed workmen focused their firepower on the riders with the powder sticks. One of the horses fell, throwing its rider, who sprinted away with a zigzagging gait, leaving his stick under the fallen horse. A second powderman ignored the gunfire, lobbed his stick well into the air, then ripped rein and galloped to catch up with the others. Twin eruptions geysered flame and thunder, the detonations rocking the site. The fallen horse was blown into the air, transformed into several large chunks of bloody meat. A flatcar was smashed into kindling and iron, and a worker using it as cover was hurled out of his boots, collapsing like an empty sack.

More powdermen veered away from the twin lines of attackers, braving furious fire to fling their sticks. Two were downed in time, but others got through, and explosions rocked the floor of the site, spewing men and matériel, spreading death and destruction—but never silencing the workers' defiant guns.

Smoothly the marauding riders melded into a single galloping file as they arrived at the front.

Flowing together without hesitation or awkwardness, they fled swiftly to the northwest and vanished noisily over scrub-brushed hillocks.

Workers boiled out from behind their blast-ravaged cover, utterly demoralized. Jessie, with Delivan grimacing beside her, surveyed the ghastly carnage of human and animal bodies. A good half of the attackers were dead, a heavy price for success. Yet the raid had been successful, unquestionably.

"Come on, Otis, we've got work to do," she said with grim urgency. "There are a lot of wounded to take care of."

Delivan nodded, exhaling heavily. "That's all that's left."

Jessie said nothing to that, not knowing what to say. She turned away, hearing faintly, from beyond the screen of boulders and rises, the drumming of many hooves receding toward the distant buttes and foothills.

Presently the engine that had hauled Delivan's coach to end-of-track was coupled to a string of flatcars, on which were loaded the badly wounded. Jessie and Delivan climbed aboard just before the train pulled out, heading back to Lobos.

Traveling the shiny rails during daylight, Jessie now could see guards posted on rises every so often. And yet as she glimpsed them, she realized how utterly impossible it was to protect every mile of track, especially after nightfall. A squad of men could creep up anywhere along the right-of-way, lay explosive charges, and block up sections of track. They could be scurrying away to another section long before the guards could reach the spot. Before Delivan could push his heavily loaded trains through with trails and ties, he'd have to repair track, and this would slow construction to a crawl.

About mid-afternoon, the emergency train eased to a halt at the Lobos depot. Immediately the depot and surrounding train yard became a loud melee of rubbernecking laborers and townsfolk, and runners went scurrying to fetch Sheriff Zeigler and the local doctor. Jessie, helping to unload the wounded on makeshift litters, spotted Ki elbowing through the crowd. She could see by his expression that he was both worried and shocked—disheveled, blood smudging her face, dirt and grit embedded in her tousled hair, she was far from her usual elegant self.

"What happened?" Ki demanded.

She smiled wearily. "Plenty."

It took Ki a while to persuade her to leave. But she truly wasn't needed now; there were many willing others who could readily handle the wounded and other loose ends. And there was much for her to do elsewhere, the first thing being to join Delivan and give their account of the attack to Sheriff Zeigler.

They convened in Delivan's private coach. "Undoubtedly the switch engine exploding and the raiders' charge were coordinated," Delivan said, concluding his and Jessie's detailed report. "That required timing, and timing in this instance has got to mean traitors in my crew."

"It had to have been arranged days earlier, the bomb or whatever detonated the switch engine rigged to explode at a definite time," Jessie added, nodding. "I can't believe the raiders would've attacked if they'd known some of the workmen were armed. That started this morning, in reaction to the bombing here yesterday."

"Thank the good Lord you did have weapons," Sheriff Zeigler growled. "But it'd been planned as a massacre. So it's come to that, has it?" He was standing motionless, his eyes seething in his rigid face. "Next they'll be slaughterin' us in our sleep. If only we could catch up with Turnbeau and his sidewinderin' gang. But we can't. They've long gone."

Shortly Jessie and Ki left the coach, Jessie eager to return to the hotel and clean up. At the front desk, the clerk handed her a letter: "Mr. Peck Adams would appreciate a conference with Miss Jessica Starbuck at four o'clock at the Imperial County Bank."

Jessie had expected something like this, and at four o'clock, bathed, freshly dressed, and accompanied by Ki, she walked down two blocks and entered the bank. Throughout the state, she had noticed, Californians seemed unaware that space was about all they had plenty of, and they had a tendency to build their structures high and narrow. The Imperial County Bank was no exception, being much like a high-ceilinged hall. It was covered with pseudo-mahogany paper and carpeted with linoleum, pitted by the hobnails of laborers and ranchers. A vault yawned, and before it was a desk inhabited by a stout man in a brown suit. Seated alongside the man was Peck Adams. Both were smoking cigars, and appeared gloomy. Also sitting there was Mrs. Rita Ballard, prim and proper, idly gazing toward the safe as she nervously rubbed her gloved hands. A clerk took Jessie and Ki inside the railing.

"Mr. Blount, our manager," he said, to introduce the stout man. "And—"

"Yes, we've all met," Jessie said, to avoid wasting time.

Adams smiled ruefully. "Investor line forms at the right."

"I'd like to be first in that line," Rita Ballard said.

"You'll have to stand on my shoulders to get there," Jessie responded.

"No fussin', ladies. You've each had a chance to look over the road and equipment. The books are here. I operate four coaches, figger fifteen hundred apiece. Figger hosses at a hundred each; that's seventy-six hundred. Figger miscellaneous equipment at another two thousand. Come to around thirteen thousand, not includin' goodwill. Knock it down to ten for depreciation."

"Clear?" Jessie asked.

"You didn't think I'd sell stock if it was, did you? I've lost money on the mail contract the last three years."

Rita Ballard kept her face turned toward the safe. "How much for fifty-one percent?"

"A million dollars. For forty-nine percent, four thousand. That would clear me."

"I'll give you forty-two," Jessie said.

"Forty-five!" Rita countered sharply. She stood, her hands clenched.

"Five."

Adams scratched his neck. "Let's have one thing clear. Stock will be nontransferable. I'll have no railroad for a partner."

Jessie's ears warmed, but Adams was regarding

Rita Ballard. "I've heard that Miss Starbuck—beggin' her pardon—is the major backer of Mist' Delivan's railroad venture. If you were to buy in, Mrs. Ballard, would you be shut of railroadin'?"

"A straight answer for a straight question. I would prevail upon you to enforce an injunction against the railroad's construction."

"And if you couldn't prevail upon me?"

"I'm sure when the time comes, I'll be able to convince you of its merits."

"Uh-huh." After a moment Adams turned to Jessie. "Suppose there's trouble. Whose side would you be on?"

Jessie's lips firmed. "I'm on the side of the Adams Stage Company. Let anyone mess with one of our stagecoaches or one of our drivers, and they've got a scrap on."

"Well, I dunno." Adams scratched his neck again. "You ain't pipin' up much, Mrs. Ballard. I'd kind of been thinking of you as my partner."

Jessie saw how pale she had gone. Her face was set. "I . . . I hoped it could be that way."

"Because I know I can count on you," Adams said. "I know your background, and I figure stagin' is a better place to be from than railroadin'."

Rita Ballard's eyes suddenly filled. "Stop it!" she said. She took a step toward Adams and then snatched her cape from a wall hook. "I've just remembered something. I—I can't do it."

Jessie smiled sweetly. "You just remembered your name was Hodge, Rita Hodge, didn't you?"

The cape fell from Rita's fingers. Her eyes were wide. Ki quietly retrieved the cape. When he straightened, Rita had walked to Adams.

"You knew, too, didn't you?"

Adams shrugged. "I'd hate to say that you look like Vernon Hodge, but there *is* something."

She turned back. At the railing gate, she faced them. "But this much is the truth: I made Daddy promise you'd make money out of it. He said you'd be paid well, in money and stock. And of course the stage line *can't* last long, Mr. Adams."

"That's where we disagree," Adams said quietly.

Rita stepped through the gate, closed it. "I'm sorry. For everything." She turned and walked briskly from the bank.

"Nice young woman," Adams sighed. "But I knew from the first she was no stagin' woman. Why, heck, she called the tugs 'thorough-braces' once! Well, if you want to throw money around, Miss Starbuck, let's get to signing papers."

Afterward, leaving the bank, they shook hands on the boardwalk. Adams smiled thoughtfully. "I'm taking you up on your offer to invest in expansion, Miss Starbuck. I figgered some time ago that in the long run the Adams Stage Lines would benefit by the M&SD. That's why I didn't hit y'all with an injunction, but on tuther hand, I ain't interested in bein' swallered up by the railroad, neither. I feel mighty lucky you came along when you did. This way, produce and livestock will be comin' in from all the towns and hamlets within hundreds of miles' radius, and Adams Line freight wagons can carry the goods to the rail depots."

"You have my word, Mr. Adams, that I'll invest in your company for its own right, and not as some minor offshoot of the railroad. We *will* be a success." Jessie meant what she said, and had every intention of following through on her oral commitment. What she did not say, but was very much on her mind, was the question of why Vernon Hodge had put his daughter up to such chicanery, and what, if anything, else he had up his land speculator's sleeve.

★

Chapter 6

Some hours later, after they had retired for the night, Ki slept on the cot with his long legs falling over the side. The canvas walls absorbed the weak candlelight. When he awoke, the candle was a curl of black twine in a puddle of grease. He lay for a while, trying to fall asleep again, and then, with a grunt, he came off the cot and poured water into the basin and rinsed his face. Refreshed, he pulled on his vest and rope-soled slippers, then left his room and walked down the hall to the lobby and adjacent barroom.

In the smoky barroom, the counter and tables hosted nondescript laborers and townsfolk, who gravitated to groups of friends and coworkers. Ki, though, spotted several knots of hardcases who kept to themselves, drank without undue show of emotion, and kept a watch on happenings around them. Almost to a man they wore common range-rider garb, faded and frayed, bristling with weapons.

Among the hardcases was a feral-looking quartet, who turned and stared at Ki with open hostility and silence—but their silence was not drunken; it was arrogant. The biggest was grossly fat, jowls sagging and potbelly bulging in rolls over his double-length gunbelt, standing braced on stout, spraddled legs. The next two were muscle-bound brutes in their late twenties with similar hog-jawed, porcine-eyed features, except that one had no left ear and the other had a nose so badly beaten that it was mashed shapeless. The fourth was as big as the others, balding, and grinned mirthlessly with lips peeled back from yellowish teeth. They were crooked teeth, with one front one grown over the other, and they gave him a pointed, coyote appearance.

And right then and there, Ki knew he was in trouble.

A tick started in the fat man's cheek, and he stepped forward belligerently. In a coarse, insulting tone, he asked, "Think you can come in here and drink with your betters, boy?"

"I'm not your boy," Ki said, his voice flat and hard. Aware that there was no way to avoid this, that they'd ride him until he groveled or fought, he added caustically, "And I don't take kindly to crowding."

The balding man laughed. "Listen to him, Rufus. The squint-eyed lackey of a female boss, warnin' men to kowtow."

"Maybe he does more'n the bitch's laundry," the man with the mashed nose said, pretending to quake in his boots. "Maybe he's her pet gunslinger."

"He ain't that," the earless man hooted. "He don't tote no gun."

The mashed-nose man scoffed, "He ain't nuthin', that's what."

"He probably thinks he is," Rufus, the fat man, said with derision. "Only he's nothing but a jackleg doin' a woman's dirty work."

There was a moment of stillness, of malignant intensity. A small crowd began gathering around, as aware as Ki that a confrontation was brewing, but ignorant of the fact that there was more to this than merely four bullies taunting an Oriental. The constant references to Jessie made it clear to Ki that they were after him to get at her, and no doubt that meant they were in the pay of whoever was wrecking the railroad.

"A jackleg," Rufus repeated sneeringly. "A jackleg hidin' behind skirts."

"If so, it's a real pleasant sensation," Ki replied sardonically. "And you ought to be glad I'm not carrying a gun. This way, even you jackals can outdraw me, when you're behind a rock and my back is turned."

Face darkening in stiff, clotted fury, Rufus lunged at Ki.

With a thin, quirked grin that masked his anger, Ki ducked Rufus's fist, catching the fat man's outflung arm and angling to drop to one knee, swinging him into *seoi otoshi,* the kneeling shoulder throw. Rufus arced through the air, over the heads of those at the adjoining table, and came down on the free-lunch counter just beyond, atop a sandwich platter and a tray of deviled eggs. He sprawled there, dazed and breathless.

Even before Rufus hit, Ki was pivoting to check what the other three were up to. The mashed-nosed man was charging with outstretched arms, as if he were tackling a drunk in an open brawl. Ki chopped the edge of his hand down on his already ruined nose; the man screamed, tears of pain springing into his eyes. Ki followed through by kicking him in the side of the knee, collapsing one side. He caught the man's right arm, crunched down on it with his elbow, and then brought his own knee into his hip.

The man—now sporting a bloody broken nose—dropped to the floor, leaving the way clear for the earless man to lash out at Ki with his wide leather belt. Ki had already seen him slide off his belt and fold it double; he had been keeping track of it peripherally until ready to deal with it. Now, stepping over the broken-nosed man, Ki caught hold of the earless man's right arm and left shoulder with his hands. Simultaneously, he moved his right foot slightly in back of the man, so that as the man began tumbling sideways, Ki was able to dip to his right knee and yank visciously. His *hizi otoshi,* or elbow drop, worked perfectly; the man sailed upside down and collapsed jarringly on top of the broken-nosed man, flattening them both to the floor.

The balding man, face purpling with rage, dove swinging at Ki. He'd launched himself from the bar while Ki was facing the man with the belt, surging in to where he was almost behind Ki, then lashing out to catch Ki unaware. He very nearly succeeded, but for Ki's glimpsing his move at the last instant.

The man swung a roundhouse haymaker, grazing against Ki's jaw before he could fully swerve aside. The blow's meaty impact sent him staggering. Wincing with pain, Ki shook his head to clear it, falling back to regain his footing.

"Stand clear, gents, give him room to hit the dirt!" the balding man called, contemptuous and confident. "Any o' you guys know I just hafta tap once to snuff a galoot's lamp out."

It was then that Ki struck back with a jolting uppercut. As skilled in unarmed combat as he was, he could've killed the man, killed him and the others with lightning speed, and a part of him was angry enough to do so. But he also realized that using methods that would appear strange and exotic to the bystanders, and leave four corpses on the barroom floor, could very easily cause serious problems with the law, lead to a long stint in jail, and foul up Jessie's mission here in Lobos. Besides, he was furious at their insulting rudeness, and he couldn't think of a better venting than to beat this lout at his own game, the crude brawl.

Ki followed the uppercut with a one-two combination, his punch starting from his shoulder and smashing in like a club. The balding man tried to jerk backward to evade the blow, but Ki had stomped his right foot atop the man's left boot, momentarily nailing the boot in place. In that moment, the man lurched, tilting off-guard and into range, and Ki kissed five knuckles square in his nose, turning the man's face into a blob of red and driving him almost to his knees. While the man was in that squatting position, Ki's left fist hammered into his chest and hurled him, squalling, back into the clustered onlookers, where he lay still.

Now Ki turned slightly as, with a yell, Rufus dove at him from the table and the earless man joined in. A backward wing of Ki's arm caught Rufus in the throat, flipping him ass-over-bootheels into a front window, which shattered in a cascade of glass shards. Rufus jackknifed outside, bowling into a trio of loafers and a pet dog napping on a plank bench. The bench upended, slintering in half and catapulting the loafers away, while by the sound of things below the window ledge, the mutt was churlishly biting Rufus.

The earless man, meanwhile, made another grab for Ki. Pivoting aside, Ki snagged him by his belt and neck and heaved him sliding down the length of the bar. The customers hastily snatched their drinks out of his path along the counter. The man plunged off into a wet mop and a bucket of dirty water, which the swamper had negligently left there after swabbing the backbar flooring.

By now the barroom was a mob scene—railroad laborers, some of the ranch hands, and most of the hardcase characters joining in the fray with gusto. Throngs crushed around, faces pressed to windowpanes, while others converged from within the hotel and out along the street. Ki ducked a straight-arm knuckler, while one of his own fists connected with a hardcase's face, dropping the man like a sack of potatoes. Glancing around, he caught sight of Rita Ballard—no, Hodge—staring, horrified, from the sidelines. Then, weaving aside, he jammed the heel of his right hand into yet another man's face. The man blundered against a stack of metal trays, toppling them and himself with a stunning clatter. Swiveling, Ki barely missed a chair whizzing past his head; it struck the backbar mirror and cracked it. One tempestuous laborer charged in, swinging a table leg. He only came partway, as Ki, springing the short distance with a leaping kick, caught him in the solar plexus. The workman careened back to slam against the bar, his makeshift club flying. But it was befitting, all in all, that Ki's last opponent should be Rufus, revived and spurred on by a couple of hardcase jokers. He vaulted onto Ki's back, encircling his throat with one arm and trying for a stranglehold. That arm was taken in an implacable grip and pulled straight out. Bending slightly, Ki hurled Rufus through the air, against the two goading hardcases. The two collapsed, legs unhinged, and fell heavily in a heap.

"B'Gawd, he downed the fat gent right smart!" Ki heard somebody declare in awe.

Another gawker guffawed. "And that one o'er there will stink o' mop water for the next month!"

Without comment Ki brushed himself off and moved toward the lobby, figuring he'd best get while the getting was good. The manager was standing off to one side, impotently gripping a side-hammer shotgun. "Somebody's gonna pay for this, or live on jail grub for a year!"

"Charge it to the railroad," Ki said wearily, moving through the surrounding crowd, vaguely aware of the men watching him. He let his hand touch the back of each chair he passed, steadyingly. Someone was beside him.

"I never, never *never* saw a man who—" Rita got a good look at Ki then and gasped. He was bloody, trickles coming from the corners of his mouth and worming from his nose. He weaved a little. "You can't go anywhere like that, Ki. You come with me. My room is just down the hall." Slipping her arm through his, she piloted him through the lobby and along the corridor.

Rita's room was a cell-like chamber not much different from Ki's. She made him sit on the edge of her bed while she lit her room's candle, cleaned his cuts, and tore up strips of cloth. Ki noted with surprise and some pleasure that her touch, for all her prissy manner, was gentle.

"There. That's as good as I can do," she said weakly, perching beside him on the bed. "Ugh, I hate blood."

Ki leaned back and grinned at her. She was so close that he could feel her warm breath against his face and smell the fragrance of her perfume. She was trembling; she stretched out a hand, placed her palm against his cheek, and stroked it gently. She said, "When I rub down, it's smooth, and when I rub up, you've got whiskers."

He reared back a bit, surprised.

She laughed throatily. "It's okay if you want me. I'm a woman—a widow, that's the truth—and you're a man . . . aren't you?"

It was that last, that purring jab of hers, that got to Ki. A lot had happened today, and he was rightfully ready for sleep, but he guessed that that was what made the difference between the sexes. He played his hand along her thigh. The muscles of her leg tightened, and Rita stopped caressing him and stared down at his hand as he stroked her thigh.

"I don't feel so brave about this as I did," she said with a sigh. "I really don't know you, don't know you at all."

"You started this."

"And you're different." She stopped talking and put her hand over his and played with his fingers, then placed them on the bosom of her dress. She was going on with it, Ki knew then, and she said, "But if I knew how much different, that'd spoil it."

Using his other hand, Ki began undoing her dress, starting at the neckline. Piece by piece he stripped her clothes off, until at last she stood and let her wispy slip blossom down around her feet.

She was naked before him, her body firm and quite broad for a woman, tapering to a slim waist and then rounding out again in slim, strong hips, her thighs curving into well-formed legs.

Ki was impressed, and hastened to be rid of his clothes. Rita watched him tug them off, then lay down on the bed, making room for him to stretch out alongside her. He glided his hand down over the smoothness of her buttocks. She raised her face and pressed her open mouth tightly against his, her hand searching down between them. He couldn't help gasping as her fingers closed around his shaft, and he ground his pelvis into her, pulling her beneath him. She opened her legs to accept him, and he plunged deep into her soft flesh.

"This is nice," she said with a sigh, straining back against him.

Ki thought it was pretty good, too. He could feel her body throb as she undulated her hips against him, her thighs pressing against his legs as her ankles snaked over and locked around his calves. He kept her too busy to talk for the next few minutes. When she did open her mouth, it was to sing out her delight, her arms wrapping tightly around his back, pulling him down against her breasts, her body following his rhythm in wild abandon. Her nails began digging at his flesh spasmodically, slithering down to knead and claw at the skin of his pumping buttocks.

More frenzied now, Rita locked her ankles firmly around him, her naked flesh slippery from the sweat of her burgeoning passion. Arching her back, she pumped up and down, undulating slowly at first, then faster and faster, until finally every sensation surging within their bodies was expelled, and they collapsed, satiated.

After a moment, she murmured, "As long as you live, you'll think of me as a liar and a cheat."

Ki shook his head. "As long as I live, Rita, I'll wonder why we had to meet this way."

She stretched her legs back so she could lie with him inside her. They dozed off, their bodies gently intertwined . . .

★

Chapter 7

"I have decided," Jessie announced at breakfast the next morning, "to go see White Water Whittaker."

Ki looked up, startled. "Are you sure? You heard what happened to Delivan's slick lawyer."

"Exactly why I feel I should give it a try. Otis Delivan is beside himself trying to manage the construction and investigate the bombings, and there's not much we can do to be of help, especially if it involves sabotage by his own people. He knows them, we don't. I wired the Circle Star, and have put all of the Starbuck field operatives in California on the job of locating the missing heirs to the Fundador land grant. Speaking of missing people, so far there's no sign of that Jimenez Linares around town, but I'm in no mood to traipse south to the Cantina Cara Dura in search of the likes of him. And the railroad's next major hurdle is bridging Blister River. Somebody has to go convince Whittaker to allow a right-of-way across his ferry landing, and sometimes a woman has an advantage in such matters."

"And sometimes not."

She smiled serenely. "Well, I suppose we'll just have to find out, won't we?"

Ki sighed the sigh of men plagued by women.

White Water Whittaker's crossing lay some distance to the northwest of Lobos, on a wagon route that the railroad was planning to parallel. The quickest way to reach it was to take the Adams stage west as far as the town of Parthenon, then hire horses and ride northerly.

After breakfast, they headed to the stage depot carrying their traveling bags. The westbound stage, which had arrived the previous evening from Calexico, was being hitched to a fresh team of horses. In the baggage room, behind the ticket office, Jessie and Ki encountered a dozen stage men listening to the driver reciting an Indian story; the driver, Tully Bierce, was an old man dressed in smoked buckskin pants and shirt, looking like an ancient buffalo hunter. Hearing Bierce, Jessie perceived something, which she mentioned privately to Ki:

"Peck Adams is living in the past, in the golden era of staging. He's surrounded himself with old men from the Oxbow Route, the Birch lines, the Central Overland. Laid end to end, the years of these men would reach back halfway to Nero."

Back outside, Peck Adams greeted them with gruff good nature. "We gen'rally leave by the clock, Miss Starbuck, not by dead reckonin'. Let me help you in."

He urged her into the coach with a big, scarred hand, then tossed in his rifle and climbed in after, closing the door. They sat discussing ways to expand the stage line, as Bierce came out and mounted the box. Ki and the expressman began passing up baggage and parcels, then Ki climbed up alongside Bierce and put a loaded Winchester across his knees. Bierce blew a loud note from a battered brass bugle. The coach sagged back on its bullhide springs and lurched forward, rolling along the main street as far as the Imperial County Bank, where Bierce reined in.

A heavy iron express box, double-locked, was carried out and placed in the body of the coach. Sheriff Zeigler superintended the loading. "There's nigh onto twenty thousand dollars in that box," he told Adams. "The bank here is responsible until it's delivered in Parthenon."

"The Adams line doesn't insure the shipments, then?" Jessie asked.

"Nope," Zeigler replied. "Y'all got to provide all necessary precautions to insure delivery, but that's as far as your responsibility goes."

"That's right, Jessie," Adams confirmed. "I've always refused to haul valuable shipments if I'm to be held responsible for possible loss. I'm just follerin' policy of most stagecoach companies."

"The time will come when all such shipments will be insured," Jessie predicted. "The bank should take out insurance on such shipments as this."

"Rates are mighty high. Rural banks don't like to spend money they figure they don't have to."

"They're liable to find themselves spending a lot more, Sheriff, if one of these shipments gets lifted on the way over."

"Wal, after the ruckus in the hotel bar last night," Zeigler said dryly, glancing up in the direction of Ki,

"I've a notion they won't be needin' to spend any on this one."

"Hope you're right," Jessie said, "but sometimes outlaws have a lot more savvy than folks give them credit for."

Shortly afterward the stage rolled out of Lobos and headed out through the gray morning sage. It made good time across the flatlands, but slowed down decidedly on the slopes of buttes and broken foothills. The six mettlesome horses had all they could do to drag the heavy vehicle up the steep inclines, and upon reaching the crests, Bierce would pull them to a halt and let them blow. Then, gathering up the reins again, he would send them down the other side into the gloom of a gorge or arroyo.

They reached Rifle Hill relay station, where a new team was latched into the traces. On they rolled, stopping for thirty minutes to lunch at Bridge Creek swing. The country was crumpling into higher hills gouged with canyons, and patches of scrawny timber began dotting the tawny rimrock. The coach swung along through dry washes and over hardscrabble ridges. Fatigue invaded the interior. For many hours now Jessie had been pummeled and beaten by the brutalities of the road, her back numb with rubbing against the horsehair cushions. Her head began to sag forward, and just as it seemed she was to get some rest, Ki's bass shout roused her and Peck Adams.

"Keep 'er rolling, Tully!" Ki yelled. "Don't let 'er stop!"

Thrusting her head out the window, Jessie saw a ruddiness on the flanks of the horses. Coming out of the turn, they swung left, out of her vision, and she had a clear view of the road. They were running into a bottleneck in a long valley, formed by a dike of sharply upstanding rocks. It was almost like a dam, rubbled at the base and sprinkled with scrub. The road burst through a gap in it, hardly twice the width of the coach itself. And the entire gap seemed to be afire with the yellow-orange flame of sunset. It fell shatteringly on Jessie. Momentarily frozen with shock, she sat there with the long barrel of her Colt resting on the ledge of the window.

Ki's rifle rammed a black bolt of sound through the air. It shattered into a scream against a rock. Bierce's voice bawled, "I can turn 'em!"

"Turn 'em, then, but don't slow!"

The coach left the graded roadbed and turned back. It was in a rutted stand of sage, running bumpily, and in the florid light, Jessie saw the face of fear on Peck Adams. Somewhere a gun cracked. She heard a bullet strike the leather belly of the coach, the deep luggage-boot behind her.

"Show those bandits something!" she yelled. She had no idea what. But she made her arm steady and gripped the window with the butt of her pistol.

Ki's Winchester broke loose again. Then of a sudden the coach was filled with thunder, as Peck Adams let fly a shot from his heavy-calibered Henry, a fifteen-shot wonder. Glancing out, Jessie saw the outlaws, jigging silhouettes against the fireball of the sun. She picked out a leader and tried to steady the pistol. It kicked at her wrist. The man kept coming. She fired again, and the man toppled, his horse shying away.

Adams lied in her ear: "Two of 'em, Jessie!"

He fired his rifle again. Riding on the front seat, he was able to fire into the outlaws without twisting.

The coach filled with bitter fumes of gunpowder. Fanning out, the outlaws showed their strength. There were at least a dozen riders armed to the teeth and coming at a full gallop. In their shaggy mustangs Jessie saw the only encouragement: A good stage team could outrun a poor saddle horse in a fair race.

Ki's carbine and Adams's rifle boomed steadily. Jessie made a crackling thunder with her revolver. A moment later the coach swerved, rocked through a sharp turn, and struck back at the road. Hastily reloading, Jessie studied another handful of outlaws who were ahead of them, directly in the stage's path. Ki's carbine opened up again. It rolled and hammered as fast as one man could pull a lever and squeeze a trigger. She saw several of the bunched outlaws take the slugs, the whole group splitting, and when the outlaws swerved away, four horses ran without riders.

The team was running wild now; Jessie could feel the surge of the stage horses' gathering strength. She pointed the barrel of her Colt at a group of riders to the right of the road. They were like wild dogs snapping at the horses' legs. She fired until the gun clicked empty, then reloaded and fired another volley. The hard spine of the attack snapped. The outlaws were in one another's way, trying to close. Jessie, Adams, and the roaring madman atop the coach kept them off balance.

Jessie fired until a slab of stone came between her and the outlaws. The coach ripped through the gap and struck into a winding, easy grade up a hillside. Watching the back road, Jessie suddenly realized the blood-fest was finished—at least for now. The hangover had set in. Dust and sunset curtained the gap in the broken stone wall.

Presently Bierce brought the horses into a trot. Ki sat alert and watchful, studying every clump of thicket and outcropping of rock as they rolled past. The outlaws might have been driven off, but that didn't mean they were through, or that another bunch weren't lurking ahead somewhere; like a hungry pack of wolves, outlaws could never be taken for granted. Ill at ease, Tully Bierce evidently held similar views.

They came to a stretch of trail that skirted the edge of a dizzy precipice for several miles. Sharp turns were frequent, and any mishap might well hurl the coach and everything connected with it into eternity. To complicate matters, the trail here had a steep downward slope. Nontheless, Bierce sent his team along at a good clip, handling them in a masterly fashion, while Ki concentrated his attention on the turns. But with a high cliff on one side and a perpendicular drop to the canyon floor more than two hundred feet below on the other, Ki decided there was little fear from owlhoots on this particular stretch.

Both he and the driver were utterly unprepared for the tragedy that struck with appalling suddenness.

The coach was careening around a curve when without warning the outer front wheel spun from the axle, hurtled over the lip of the trail, and vanished into the depths below. Down went the axle, striking the ground with prodigious force. The coach reeled wildly, the inner front wheel coming clear off the ground.

Tully Bierce was flung from the seat like a stone from a slingshot. His yell of fright thinned to a shriek of abject terror as he cleared the lip of the precipice and hurtled downward. Ki barely saved himself by an iron grip on the railing that surrounded the seat. Instinctively he grabbed for the reins, which were trailing over the dashboard of the box, and got them the instant before they would have flipped to the ground.

As the crippled coach bounced and thundered at their heels, the terrified horses bolted. Wild with fright, they fled madly down the steep and winding trail, skidding around the turns, leaping, floundering, straining every nerve and muscle to escape the horror that crashed and bounded at their heels. With each beat of the sagging axle on the ground, the coach lurched and reeled crazily, on the verge of an upset a hundred times a minute. It slammed against the cliff face with a force that threatened to smash it to splinters, slithered toward the yawning gulf, zigzagged back and forth. Once the outer rear wheel was actually over the lip, and spun crazily in empty air for a split second before slamming down on the trail once more.

With every once of his strength, Ki fought to get the frantic horses under control. As the coach crashed against the cliff face, he was all but knocked from the box. The terrific jar of the dragging axle meeting solidly with a projecting boulder hurled him forward against the dashboard. Luckily the impact was too much for the boulder and rooted it from its bed instead of turning the coach over on top of the horses.

Around a hairpin turn wheeled the bounding vehicle, the horses leaning far over and keeping their footing by a miracle. The veins stood out on

Ki's forehead like cords. The stout box creaked and groaned as he braced his feet against the dashboard and dragged back on the reins, fearing they would snap under the terrible strain put upon them. Powerful as he was, though, he could not match strength with the six maniac horses with the bits in their teeth. He realized that sooner or later he would, momentarily at least, lose control and the whole equipage, with him, Jessie, and Peck Adams, would hurtle into the gulf that yawned for them hungrily. He gambled everything, their lives included, on a desperate chance.

Directly ahead, a shoulder of rock jutted out sharply from the main mass of the cliff. As the raging team bore down upon it, Ki gauged the distance and put every particle of his strength in one mighty pull that swerved the horses sharply to the right.

The team flashed past the shoulder, the inside leader rasping against the stone and all but losing its footing. But the remaining front wheel did not miss. It slammed against the unyielding stone with a force that hurled Ki from the seat to land on the back of the off-wheeler, from whence he rolled to the ground to lie with one foot dangling over the gulf.

The wheel flew to splinters, the ponderous iron axle snapped like a straw; but the progress of the coach was halted as if by a mighty hand. With both front wheels gone, the body fell forward and jammed against the cliff shoulder. The stout leather traces held and the horses were swept off their feet in a squalling, kicking tangle, the breath knocked out of them, and with it their urge to keep on running.

His head spinning, sweat pouring down his face and soaking his body, every nerve and muscle shaking from intolerable strain, Ki staggered upright and across to the coach. "Jessie! Adams! You okay in there?"

From within, Jessie answered in a shaky voice, "We're breathing."

"Of course we're breathing," Adams added hoarsely. "It's all I can do right now."

Ki staggered over to the horses then, calling soothingly as he took out a knife and commenced cutting them free from the tangle of harness. They regained their feet, snorting and trembling, and huddled against the cliff, too exhausted and nerve-shattered to seek escape. By then Jessie had managed to climb from the sagging coach body. Adams followed on wobbly legs, gripping his rifle and breathing in great gulps of air. Glancing up, Ki saw his Winchester hanging between the seat and the guardrail. Absently he reached up and got the carbine. Then, tucking the gun under his arm, he joined the other two as they leaned against the coach, getting their breath back and steadying their nerves.

"Are you sure you're all right?" he asked them.

"I reckon," Adams replied, wincing. "A twister of a headache. Other'n that, nothing particular feels snapped or busted."

"What luck," Jessie said. Luck. That unpredictable factor, she thought, stepping to the lip of the precipice. She stared up the canyon, where lay the lifeless, broken body of the driver. It was bad luck for them—especially for Tully Bierce—that the stage had lost a wheel, and unbelievably good luck that everyone else had come through uninjured. How do you gauge it? How do you figure it? Shaking her head, Jessie was about to step back to the coach when she detected movement in the brush several hundred yards up the canyon in the direction from which they had come.

"Riders!"

A body of horsemen rode out of the brush, their eyes fixed on the rim of the cliff.

"Reckon they saw that tightrope act we were doing up here," Adams muttered, his gaze on the approaching horsemen. "Do you think they're them owlhoots who—"

Suddenly he leapt back from the cliff, ducking down at the same instant. A bullet screeched over his head and slammed against the cliff face. Others followed it. He hurled himself to the ground, the Henry thrust out in front of him. Jessie and Ki sprang for the rocks, bringing their weapons to bear.

Smoke wisped from the Winchester's muzzle. The boom of a report echoed the crackling of Jessie's revolver and the throaty report of the Henry. One of the approaching riders threw up his arms and spun from the saddle like a tumbler performing his act. A second man reeled, clutched at the saddle horn for support, and fell forward on his horse's neck.

The three gun muzzles shifted slighty, spurted smoke. More yells of pain drifted up from the canyon floor. The horses of the approaching men were milling in wild confusion, their riders desperately fighting to turn them. Another moment and they were scudding back the way they had come.

The trio of defenders sent streams of lead hissing after them. They did not cease pulling triggers until the last of the band had vanished into the brush.

Then, eyes still fixed on the fringe of growth, they rapidly reloaded. For some moments they watched the distant leaves and branches. Then Adams lowered his Henry and stood up.

"Reckon they got plenty," he muttered.

"I see it now," Jessie said. "This wasn't an accident after all."

Adams shook his head. "Yeah, they must've figured to pick the express box out of the smashup down there in the gully."

Turning, Jessie eyed the wrecked coach thoughtfully. Holstering her revolver, she stooped over the axle from which the wheel had spun free. As she traced the threads that should have held in place the nut that secured the wheel to the axle, the concentration furrow between her brows deepened.

"Peck, come here and take a look."

Adams came over. "Them pizenous skunks!"

Ki, too, inspected the axle. "Maybe we shouldn't let them know we're on to this," he suggested. Jessie and Adams agreed. Selecting a conveniently sized boulder, then, Ki deliberately smashed the threads out of shape, just as they could have been damaged by the axle bumping over the stones in the course of its wild careen along the trail. Next he smashed the coach door with the boulder and dragged out the iron express box.

The exhausted coach horses were still huddled against the cliff. With straps cut from the harness, Ki, Jessie, and Peck Adams lashed the box to the back of one of them. Then they took one of the reins, knotted it to the animal's bit ring, and passed it through the bit rings of two other horses. Mounting the three remaining horses, they headed down the trail toward Parthenon, Ki leading the harnessed horses behind them.

This was the strange procession that, a few hours later, startled the eyes of the astonished folks of Parthenon.

Peck Adams directed the way straight to the Parthenon branch of Imperial County Bank. When the flabbergasted bank manager arrived from his home, Adams cut the express box loose and, with Ki, carried it into the bank.

"I'd like a receipt for this," he told the manager. "And we'd best roust whatever passes for a lawdog hereabouts," he added. "He'll hafta ride to the canyon below the cliff trail and pick up poor ol' Tully Bierce, or what's left of him. He'll find a few punctured gents a little farther down the gulch. Now, I gotta get to my stage depot. There's a chore for the fellers there to do, too."

After Adams had recounted the mishap on the trail, a crew set out from the depot to repair and bring in the damaged coach. He turned to Jessie, then, smiling wearily. "It's been a day, and it's late. I'll find you and Ki rooms. The Desert Inn is good. Oh—and Jessie?"

"Yes?"

"You handle a Colt with the best, if'n I do say so. We'll take on the Apache nation sometime."

"Not if I can help it. Good night, Peck."

★

Chapter 8

Jessie and Ki spent the night at the Parthenon Desert Inn. Rarely had they slept in a rooming house with a fancier name, or in dirtier rooms, with more tin-patched rat holes. After eating at a nearby cafe, they went to the stage depot, where Peck Adams provided them with two saddlers—a pair of tough roan geldings. Adams himself was staying to see that Tully Bierce got a proper funeral, and then was going to continue on west, visiting the line's depots and relay stations to explain about Jessie's investment and their plans for expansion. So it was here that he parted company with Jessie and Ki, who headed north out of town, toward the Coyote Mountains and Blister River.

The trail carried ruts left by wagons and buggies, but mainly it appeared to be a cattle trail—one rustlers might use, Jessie reckoned, to move herds down to Mexico. They rode all day, and camped at sunset out of sight and sound of the trail, picketing their horses in a swath of grass and screening their bedrolls behind a bramble thicket. Unwilling to risk a fire, they ate a cold supper. Night eased down around them, stealing across the grama, turning the rocks from burnt ocher to dark blue. Exhausted, they slept dreamlessly yet lightly, never fully unconscious.

Next morning, they followed the trail as it skirted the foothills of the Coyotes. Around noon they came to where the trail intersected another trail, this one more along the lines of a formal wagon road. Joining it, they headed northwesterly, the road meandering across the heat-blasted foothills, through a maze of connecting arroyos and ravines, leading into a broad rise of uplands textured with sagebrush, creosote bushes, juniper patches, and scraggly windswept conifers. The sun was low in the west when Jessie noticed a musty tingling in her upper nostrils, a sort of mildew odor, and it occurred to her that they must be nearing the Blister River.

Presently the road veered along the rim of a gorge. The gorge was steeply sloped, hopper-shaped, and heavily overgrown, with the bed of a river serving as its floor. Here was not the site of White Water Whittaker's ferry crossing; the Blister cascaded through a series of rapids in a foaming, surging rush. The crossing would have to be somewhere ahead, where the river would be calmer and not compressed between sheer walls. They moved on, heading upstream, flanking the nearby eastern bank, though often bouldered outcroppings and thick bushes in between hid the noisy tributary from view.

A few miles later they were coming to a stretch where the banks began dipping in a rounded slope, when they heard the rattle of gunfire close ahead. Without a word, Jessie kicked her gelding into a gallop. Ki launched himself after her, following her through a concealing screen of trees and underbrush. Voices could be heard, bellowing in anger, but mostly the crash of guns echoed back at them. Suddenly Jessie reined in hard.

"Ki—look!"

Simultaneously with Jessie's call, Ki's sharp eyes caught sight of what had brought her to a quick halt. They were on the trail-indented ledge of a deeply eroded cliff overlooking the river. Below was a broad clearing that ran on a shallow incline to the Blister, now wide and smooth. On the river was a barge of unbarked logs, and a ferryman's shanty, with moldy gunnysacking at its windows, which looked as though it had been stacked up from driftwood. It had a stick-and-clay chimney showing a straight-up hairline of smoke. It wasn't exactly the kind of an enterprise you'd use gunwolves to fight over.

But four hunkering men were fanned out behind the rocks and brush, eyes and weapons trained on the shanty. The volley of shots had died, and in the hush that followed, Jessie and Ki heard a voice shout out—a voice that, much to Ki's surprise, he recognized as that hardcase Rufus's foghorn bawl: "We can keep you penned in till hell freezes over, Whittaker! You're bogged down, and you orter come out and get it over with!"

"Hell I will, you warty-faced hound!" a gravelly voice yelled. There was the squeak of door hinges, then: "Do your damndest, you thievin', lily-livered polecats! I'm nestin' plump, with plenty fodder for my ol' Peabody!"

Jessie and Ki now could see a white-bearded, white-maned old man standing in the doorway, dressed in a blue flannel shirt and overalls and a pair of tallowed boots; short, paunchy, bowlegged, with a pair of hard green eyes and a hide as weathered as old leather. Defiantly he clutched at the ready a vintage single-shot Peabody rifle. Uneasiness seemed to ripple through the four besiegers now, at the mention of the .45/70/480 rimfire cartridges used to stoke the gun.

"You won't torch that cannon at us," Rufus blustered with a touch of scorn. "Now, c'mon out and stop bein' stupid!"

"It's too late for that!" Pausing, Whittaker lifted a gallon jug to his white-bearded lips and began drinking thirstily, making sure to keep one hard green eye on his attackers. "Ahhh!" he sighed in satisfaction, setting the jug down. Fortified by a few swallows of his own potent moonshine whiskey, he bellowed, "If'n you want me, try gettin' me, you suck-egg stinkin' buckets of sheep dip! I'll slice your ears off for dessert and feed the vultures yet!"

Rufus cursed. "Drive him in and flat, boys! Cut that damn shack of his in two and bring it down 'round his fat head!"

Gun thunder rolled again, as repeaters and revolvers blistered the shanty's walls and hastily slammed door. Then the barrel of the Peabody poked out a window, erupted with a roar, and one of the men with Rufus let out a bleat as over an ounce of lead plucked his hat away.

"Good God, they'll kill Whittaker!" Jessie shouted, hauling her carbine from its saddle scabbard. "We can't let them do that! We need his right-of-way!"

Wild cursing went up from the four in the brush, as they caught sight of two riders spurring down the trail to the clearing, sunlight glinting on their carbine barrels. A spate of gunshots bracketed Jessie and Ki with lead as the attackers hastily changed targets to fight off the unexpected charge. Braving the fire, Jessie and Ki aimed and triggered with precision. One of the gang—the balding man with the coyote teeth—threw up his hands with a death scream and rolled soddenly down the clearing slope toward the river. The Peabody erupted again. Facing the peril of being caught in a crossfire, Rufus and his two remaining cohorts chose to retreat, racing off through the brush toward where their mounts were tethered in a bunch.

Dusty-faced but smiling, Jessie and Ki swung astride their horses when the last of the retreating gunmen vanished around the far end of the clearing. The men, besides being thwarted in their scheme to kill Whittaker, had left one of their number for buzzard bait.

The door opened again and Whittaker came out, his hard green eyes, deep-set under ragged gray brows, looking over Jessie and Ki. "I don't know who the hell you are," he said, "or where you come from, ner why. But you done me some good." He took an extra gander at Jessie, and his features relaxed into a broad grin. "My, if you ain't got a hull worthy of a clipper."

"Mr. Whittaker!" Jessie chided, then introduced herself and Ki.

Instead of shaking hands, Whittaker offered them his jug—then, frowning, he took it back, squinted into it, upended it, and swore under his breath.

"Empty. Dagnabit, now I gotta go fetch some more." He glanced around, trying to disguise his nervous concern. "You're, eh, you're welcome to tag along, if'n you're a mind to."

They were of a mind to.

Clapping on a broad-brimmed hat and collecting his horse, a shaggy sorrel, Whittaker led the way into the flanking brush. There they joined a path, an easily overlooked path, no more than a single-file ribbon that kept close to the contours of the land, rarely along rises, but through clefts and hollows. Whittaker kept quiet while they loped westward along its wandering course, and neither Jessie nor Ki pressed him, keeping mum as well. The sun lowered westward, setting in a fiery glow. Dusk settled in. The shadows grew longer. Eventually the silence was too much for Whittaker.

"Them scummy, low-down, good-for-nothin' hounds," Whittaker abruptly said, "was fixin' to kill me."

"Yeah?" Jessie grinned.

White Water Whittaker cut her a sharp look. "I was doin' all right, young lady," Whittaker declared with halfhearted stubbornness. "Doin' all right." Then his voice became a growl, laden with suspicion. "What made you save my neck? How much do I owe you? Name it!"

"Take it easy."

"Name your price, young lady!"

"Your river crossing."

Their eyes met and held. Like a hard, hurting hand grip.

"I'd as soon be dead," Whittaker said obstinately, "as to give up all I got."

Jessie nodded. "I'm taking away nothing from you."

Whittaker shook his head. "I never taken a pardner in my life. I'll pay you what it's worth. But I'll sell out to no man—or woman. Ner give any man on earth a pardnership."

"I need the crossing. I'm gambling for it."

"I know who you is, but *what* are you?"

"That doesn't matter much right now. We can take it up later if you want my pedigree."

White Water Whittaker's hard green eyes under the slanted hat brim kept shooting covert glances at Jessie, as if the old rascal were trying to figure how to seduce her into submission. He finally yanked his hat off and scratched his uncombed shock of white hair. "High-handed, ain't yuh, gal? Like you was used to gittin' what you went after. I'll deal with you. You take one side o' the Blister, I'll keep t'uther. We'll slide that ferryboat back and forth and make 'er pay. I'll squeeze the drippin's of white Lightnin' outa the still, and your friend there, Ki, he can peddle a jug now and then on yonder side of the river. The catfish is bitin', and we'll stretch a trotline across from bank to bank with about fifty hooks hung onto the short lines. Now an' then some of the boys that's heard the owl hoot will come along. They pay big for little favors. Me on my side of the river, an' you two on yours . . ."

White Water Whittaker talked himself out under the level golden-green stare of Jessie. She was grinning flatly. "We'll make our dicker later," she told Whittaker. She wasn't much interested in peddling moonshine whiskey or running a ferryboat, but she wasn't saying what her plans were, except that she needed both sides of the Blister River crossing. And she and Ki had come a long ways to bargain for it. Apparently, judging by the tone Whittaker was taking, she was far from the only one interested in his operation.

"Who else wants your crossing?" she asked.

That brought a snarl from Whittaker. He said every damned outfit in that part of the country had tried, at some time or another, to buy him out or run him out. Fact was, he said, it would be hard to name anybody that didn't want his crossing, with the fertile river bottomlands and the broken badlands behind for a winter range. Take both sides of the crossing and the land included and you had as fine a ranch as the area had to offer, winter or summer.

Jessie grew fully alert then, all her senses sharpened. Ahead, against the backdrop of dusky gray sky, she spotted a flickering glow rising from somewhere in the blue-black terrain. "Looks like a fire yonder."

"It can't be a grass fire," Ki reckoned. "Not here."

"My place!" Whittaker howled, and booted his sorrel into a mad gallop.

There was a night breeze coming from the river. It carried the unmistakable smell of burning wood. Then they saw the angry yellow glare of the blaze. A hoarse, animal-like cry ripped from the old man's throat. His horse was covering the ground at a long, tireless lope. The old man's Peabody was in his hand, and Jessie and Ki slid their carbines from their saddle scabbards.

They got there too late to put out the fire that was burning Whittaker's cabin and one of his sheds. By the light of the flames they could see the wreckage of his whiskey still. It had been smashed into a shapeless mass, the barrels of mash chopped with an axe until they were no more than splintered bits of hardwood staves and twisted hoops. The sweet-sour stench of the spilled mash mingled with the smell of blazing lumber. The old renegade would have ridden into the glow of the fire to fight it, but for Ki grabbing his bridle reins.

"Want to get ambushed?"

"Damn 'em! Damn their picayune souls!" Whittaker rasped. "Lemme git to 'em!"

"We'll get to them," Jessie said, "from behind. They can't have beat us here by much, so they can't have gotten far. For the river, that's where I think they'd flee. Come on, we'll fight for what we've got left!"

They headed for the river. About four hundred yards ahead they sighted three riders galloping in the same direction. Without checking the speed of her horse, Jessie stood in her stirrups and shot over the ears of her mount at the riders as they hit the river and started across. Her big roan gelding had outrun Whittaker's sorrel at least fifty yards, so that Whittaker was behind and to one side. But he and Ki saw one of those escaping riders sway in his saddle as his horse took the river. And they saw the lithe young woman in front ride on to the river's edge, to the fringe of willows there, and dismount.

The river looked black even in the moonlight. Log snags driving downstream took on the appearance of men swimming their horses. Jessie stood there at the edge of the willows, and now and then her carbine would crack, spewing flames. Whittaker and Ki rode up at a lope and swung from their saddles.

Breathing heavily, his Peabody gripped in his gnarled hands, Whittaker wheezed, "Where?"

"I got one," Jessie said. "But it's so dark out there I can't spot them. But I saw that one man fall off his horse out there in the fast channel. His horse went on across. We might as well ride back and keep the sparks from setting anything more afire." Jessie spoke quietly—as quietly, Whittaker remarked to Ki later, as a schoolmarm at a prayer meeting.

They headed back for the burning ranch. Ki rode around the place first, making a circle. Then when he was certain that all the men who had set the fire were gone, he and Whittaker and Jessie got wet gunnysacks and fought the sparks that landed on the barn, hayrick, outhouse, and sheds, and it was gray dawn when they finally got a rest.

All three of them were fire-blackened and their clothes burned in places. Their hair and Whittaker's whiskers were singed, their eyes red-lidded, bloodshot slits. Sweat ran across their blackened faces in tiny rivulets, and they were limp with fatigue. But the structures had been saved. Whittaker said the cabin wasn't too great a loss, that it was an old whiskey-soaked bachelor boar's nest that hadn't been swept out in months. And he'd been putting off repairing and improving his still anyhow.

"You couldn't have bought my crossing," he croaked, grinning, "or you couldn't have crowded me into it. But Miz Starbuck, if you want a pardnership in what I got left, it's yourn free of charge!"

The old man kept his grub supply along with his whiskey makings in a side hill dugout. While Jessie got breakfast over a camp fire, the old man took care of their horses and his sorrel. Then he poked around in the charred and smoking ruins of his cabin with a pitchfork, cussing into his white beard when he located the burned remnants of some treasured object. After a while he began scouting off in different directions, ignoring Jessie's call to grub. The old moonshiner was making the rounds of his numerous caches where he had hidden jugs of his whiskey. He fetched back a jug and said that the damned sons hadn't located a single cache. And back in the hills he had several barrels of whiskey hidden, a four-to-five-year supply for his trade and own use.

Jessie declined his offer for a drink, and Ki sipped cautiously of the potent shine. And when they had eaten, Jessie said she wanted to cross the river, just to see what was on the yonder side. None of them was forgetting the three night riders who had tried to burn out White Water Whittaker. None of them doubted that the three were the survivors of the four who had tried to gun down Whittaker at his ferry crossing. Only Jessie and Ki knew, however, that the men were the ones who'd braced Ki in the Belle of Lobos barroom—and who, Ki still felt sure, were somehow tied in with Delivan's railroad troubles.

The three night riders were probably down to two now, considering the one Jessie had dumped into the river. But the remaining duo could well be lying over in the brush with their guns ready. "Or up in them rocks there," Whittaker said, pointing to a bouldered rise just up from the opposite bank. "They could lie in behind them and pick us off easy." Crossing the Blister in broad daylight was risky. Whittaker had an old, leaky, klinker-built rowboat available; but, he growled, only a fool would hazard crossing in that and making a plain target of himself.

Ki asked about the drift of the current from the bend about two miles above them. Whittaker said the current was swift around the bend and that the channel angled across to a long willow-covered sandbar. Ki nodded. "That's just about the way I figured, but I wanted to be sure." He told Jessie and Whittaker his plans. Whittaker said it was a plain damn fool thing to tackle but that Ki looked big enough and growed-up enough to know his own mind.

"You two bush up in the willows on this side," Ki told them, "with your sights raised to the last notch. If I'm sighted and shot at, maybe you can get in a little target practice."

Ki went on to the foot of the river, keeping to the brush until he had reached the bend. He found a cottonwood log that had been hung up in the brush. It took half an hour to locate another log about the same size. By then Whittaker had returned from a fast ride back to his burned-out property, where he had scrounged up some big nails and a hammer. They fastened the two logs together. Ki stripped naked, rolled his clothes in a ball, and with a saddle rope lashed the load along with his carbine to the log raft. Then he shoved the raft into the swift, muddy river and swam behind it, hanging onto the tail end to steer it. He had plastered his long black hair with river mud, figuring that it would take a pair of sharp eyes to spot him as he went down on the swift current, angling for the west bank and the sandbar that was covered with a heavy growth of willows and underbrush.

Ki landed almost exactly where he had calculated. He got his clothes and carbine and slipped into the brush. His clothes had gotten wet in places from the lapping of the water. He dried the water from his carbine and wiped himself partly dry with his shirt. Then he dressed and made his way through the willows and brush in a detour that brought him around the bouldered rise—the most logical place for the night riders to hunker in, assuming that had been their notion.

It had been. Ki spotted three saddled horses grazing, bridle reins dragging. A small, smokeless camp fire was smoldering. Two men were squatting around the fire, lackadaisically poking at the coals or pouring tin cups of coffee from the pot warming on some glowing kindling. Ki grinned flatly as he recognized Rufus and one of the two younger men. And down near the riverbank he could see the dark outline of a third man sitting cross-legged on the ground behind a brush patch, watching the east bank, a saddle carbine across his lap.

Ki crouched in behind a large boulder and watched the men. His was a waiting game now, and he played it with all the patience he had. It seemed hours before Rufus stood up, dusted himself off, and called to the man down at the riverbank. "C'mon and eat, Fred. Ben will spell you. See anything of 'em?"

"Nary a sign of nobody o'er there, Rufus." The man called Fred came up from the riverbank, his carbine in the crook of his arm.

Ki waited until the three men were standing close together. Rufus was wearing a wide-brimmed, high-crowned hat. Ki lined up his carbine sights on the top of the high-crowned Stetson and squeezed the trigger.

The burly Rufus ducked as if he were dodging a thrown rock. All three men gripped their guns.

"Drop your guns and reach high. I won't shoot to miss the next time. Try to rabbit and I'll kill you. Drop them!"

Rufus's beefy red face was mottled now, spotting with gray. The younger man named Ben snarled, "I don't throw away my iron for no damned man!"

Ki's carbine cracked again. The .44–40 slug struck Ben in the right shoulder, knocking him sideways and around. His gun dropped from his hand, and his lean face turned a muddy gray color. "Don't shoot me no more!"

Rufus and the other man, Fred, dropped their guns. Ki told them to keep their hands up and to turn and walk away from the three carbines and pistols on the ground.

"A passel of two-bit sneak-thieves who snitch trinkets out of ol' ladies' handbags," Ki sneered, just to drop their fighting spirit another notch. "You, Ben, you were the gent who got shot last night when you were making your getaway from White Water Whittaker's place? Loosen that tongue of yours, or I'll bust your other wing!"

"Don't shoot me no more. Yeah, yeah, but I only got grazed."

"Y'all fell down on the job. Your orders were to kill Whittaker, me, and Jessie Starbuck when we rode into the light of the fire. How much was Rufus here paying you two vermin?"

"I didn't hire 'em!" Rufus yelped. "I never had a damn thing to do with any part of anything." He was wheezing now like a pair of old bellows. His heavy right hand was moving toward the inside pocket of his leather jacket. Easing also, Ki figured, toward the second gun the big man undoubtedly packed in a shoulder holster under the jacket.

"Unless you're certain, Fatso," Ki said quietly, "that this is your lucky day, don't pull that sneak gun . . . You, Fred, reach in with your left hand and get that gun he's packing. Throw it away. Then tie up that shoulder of Ben's before he bleeds to death. Move there, Fred!"

Rufus wheezed profanely. Ki, straightening up so that his head and shoulders showed above the rocks, grinned wolfishly as the lanky Fred removed Rufus's second gun, a hammerless .32 pistol, and tossed it to the ground. Fred immediately went to work stopping the flow of blood from Ben's bullet-smashed shoulder. Ben was gray with pain and looking wobbly in the knees.

Ki said he'd forgotten all about his partners—that Whittaker and Miss Starbuck would be having fits and little 'uns across the river. "So just trail down to the banks of the river, gents." He herded the three men to the bank, halted them, and yelled across the river. "Hey, Jessie! White Water! Come on over! I've got something special to show you!"

Whittaker barked out a profane reply. He wanted to know what the shooting was about and what the hell did he mean, keeping a man and a lady bushed up and sweatin'. Then he was shoving his skiff into the water, helping Jessie in, and rowing across. The old rascal could handle a boat in that swift current, his powerful arms and shoulders moving the oars like they were matchsticks, and he took a riverman's experienced advantage of every twist in the swift current. They were across in a few minutes. After Jessie got out, Whittaker hauled his rowboat up on the bank and picked up his Peabody.

"I'll cut out their gizzards and make 'em eat 'em!" Whittaker bellowed, stomping toward Ki and the three men. "I'll roast their livers over a fire and *whup!*"

The *whup!* was in startled response to Rufus, who of a sudden took it upon himself to dive from the high embankment into the river with a loud splash.

Jessie stood there on the bank, her carbine in hand, watching the swirling, treacherous river with its dangerous undercurrents and whirlpools, its drifting snags. It took a good swimmer to handle himself in the Blister River here—as she had witnessed when Ki had crossed—and Rufus was handicapped by the sodden weight of his clothes and boots and filled cartridge belt. And, as she watched, she realized that either Rufus had struck something underwater and was hanging there drowning, or he was swimming below the surface and letting the swift current carry him downstream. That would take real swimming.

A boot floated to the surface. Then a half-submerged thing that could have been a leather jacket.

"Could be him," Whittaker growled. He lifted his rifle, pointing at something a couple of hundred yards downstream.

Jessie knocked the barrel up a split second before the gun roared. "Could be him, White Water," she said, smiling at the blazing anger in the old whiskey peddler's hard green eyes. "If he can make it, let him go. Rufus has guts aplenty."

White Water Whittaker growled into his white beard. They all stared downstream toward the man who was clinging to an old cottonwood branch that was driving down the river with the current. They could see the big man crawl into its foam-laden branches and disappear. Rufus had swum underwater with the swift current, all right, holding his wind, shedding his leather jacket and cartridge belt and getting rid of at least one boot below the surface, coming up for air far downstream and then grabbing himself passageway on a big old cottonwood snag. That took guts and river savvy.

Whittaker admitted it reluctantly. "Most cowhands can't swim. Can't handle theirselves or their horses in bad water. But he done it, tho' that pot-gutted big son shore made a purty mark to shoot at."

"Rufus is only a hired hand," Jessie said. "Like these two hombres. These are the two out of four left that set fire to your place, partner. They're your meat from here on."

The man named Ben was suffering now. His partner Fred had bandaged the wounded shoulder, and though it was a clean flesh wound, the man was still suffering. His face was beaded with sweat and his hair was wet with it and pain scared his bloodshot eyes. Fred was scared now too—scared of the look in the hard green eyes of old White Water Whittaker.

"I got a mind," Whittaker said, "to gut-shoot 'em both and shove their carcasses into the river. There was a big pitcher in my cabin. A real paintin' of the Custer Massacre. With the names of the soldiers an' Injuns. Scalpin' an' whatnot. Gen'ral Custer standin' there, an ol' cap-an'-ball six-shooter in his hand . . . It a pitcher put out by Anheuser Busch Brew'ry. Hell, a man could look at 'er a winter night an' study 'er like a book, and these barstards—er, excuse me, ma'am—burnt 'er up, to 'er gilted frame. I got a mind to gut-shoot—"

"Better," Jessie said, "if we find out who paid these gents. I'll get you another Custer picture. I know a few folks at Anheuser Busch, and I'm sure they'll supply you another picture for the cabin we'll make these men build. They burned one down. They'll build a new cabin. And until Ben gets well, his partner Fred will do the work of two men. . . . Or would you two fire-starters rather take the jump you watched Rufus take?"

Fred was begging now, with his eyes and croaking voice. He sunk down on his knees before Whittaker, Jessie, and Ki.

"Work the yellow seat outta him," the wounded Ben said. "What is it you want outta me? I'm over a barrel. But I won't beg or whine."

Whittaker, without any more warning than a deep-throated snarl, went into action. The wounded Ben and the scared Fred went over the clay bank and into the water. They splashed out of sight under the water, then came up twenty or thirty feet downstream, sodden, gasping, half-drowned, pawing at the water with their hands.

"Who're you workin' fer?" Whittaker raged. "Tell it an' I'll fish you out."

"Tornado!" gasped the panicky, half-drowned Fred.

"Tornado Turnbeau!" Ben's voice was a snarl. He was trying to keep afloat, his one good arm splashing water.

White Water Whittaker and Ki ran down to where the rowboat was pulled up on the bank. They shoved it into the water. Ki grabbed Fred's thick hair as he was going under for the last time and yanked him up and over into the boat. Then he hauled Ben more carefully in over the stern of the boat. Whittaker spat tobacco juice into the water and swung the boat back to the sandy bank.

They laid the waterlogged Fred across a big cottonwood log and worked on him until he was vomiting water. Whittaker returned to the boat and came back with a jug of moonshine whiskey, a drink of which he gave Ben, who was shivering and shaking, his yellow teeth chattering.

"I never burnt that Custer pitcher," Ben said. "I taken it and some other stuff outta your cabin. Hid it right nearby, aimin' to claim it for myself someday."

Once he started, Ben talked through chattering teeth for the reward of another drink of that potent moonshine whiskey. But there actually wasn't much he could tell that Jessie and Ki didn't already know or surmise. Turnbeau was out to stop the railroad, because if he didn't, eventually the mere presence of the M&SD would stop him by bringing in homesteaders and, ultimately, forceful law and order. Turnbeau was not alone in wanting to end the railroad's incursion into his domain, but Ben had no idea who his silent partner or partners were, or what their motives were.

When even Whittaker was satisfied that Ben knew no more than he was telling, he asked Jessie, "What'll we do with these two fire-settin' arsenic things?"

"Arson." Jessie corrected. "Not arsenic."

"Arsenic er arson, what's the difference? They burnt me out. I'm kickin' 'em back into the river."

Jessie shook her head. "I've a better notion." She fed Fred and Ben a couple of big drinks. Then she got their horses and a big gelding that belonged to Rufus. "Now, get into the rowboat," she ordered Fred and Ben. "White Water will row you across. Ki and me will swim the three horses behind us."

When they were all back on the eastern side, Jessie and Ki soaked to their skins, Jessie fixed her eyes on Ben and Fred. "I just sighted Rufus coming ashore on this side. Take his horse to him. Then the three of you ride on to Tornado Turnbeau's camp. When you get there, tell Turnbeau that Whittaker and his partner sent you back. Tell him that if he wants us, to come for us himself, with all the help he can muster. There'll just be Whittaker and Ki and myself waiting here to greet him and his outfit."

"Git, you pair o' fire-eatin' arsenics!" snarled Whittaker. "You got my pardner's orders. Tell Tornado to come 'n' git me!"

After Fred and Ben had ridden off down the river to pick up Rufus and take the fighting talk to Tornado Turnbeau, Whittaker, Jessie, and Ki retrieved their horses and rode back to Whittaker's burned-out ranch. En route, Whittaker remarked, "You're sure a high-handed fire-eater, Ki. An' Miz Starbuck, lemme include you in sayin' fellers like y'all don't run in bunches . . . You sure'n hell matched us a fight with Turnbeau. He'll fetch his outfit, guaranteed. It'll be a rumpus, young lady."

All they could do was agree with him.

And then wait.

Whittaker did not wait peacefully. Restless and uneasy, he dug up a jug of his oldest shine and complained that it tasted like river water. He went out to his small barn—which, considering the hay in its loft, had miraculously missed being burned—and talked to his ornery horse. He came away shaking his head and muttering. Then he rigged a troll line with fifty hooks, baited the hooks, and ran it across to the west bank. Instead of lazing away the time until a fish bit a hook, the cranky old river renegade kept pacing around, his bushy, ragged brows knit in a scowl and a haunted look in his hard green eyes.

Jessie tended to her horse and cleaned her pistol and carbine. After drying out his clothes, Ki settled cross-legged in the shade of a giant cottonwood. His arms crossed, he cupped his hands over his ears and purposely slowed his breathing. He remained thus, relaxing and meditating.

About sundown, Whittaker pulled in a ten-pound fish and skinned it, and they broiled it on a bed of coals and had a feast. Afterward, Whittaker, still restless, wandered grumbling into the brush to relieve himself. Within a minute he was rushing back out, fumbling at the buttons of his pants. "Yonder they come!" He grabbed hold of his jug and took a healthy snort of moonshine whiskey. "By the hell, I always said I'd never die of old age!" He grinned as he tallied the riders coming down the ridge toward the burnt-out ranch. "Let's have at them!"

With dusk descending, they locked the barn doors and climbed to the loft and waited. They saw Rufus scattering a handful of men into the brush. They watched another man, brutish in size and demeanor, directing another dozen or fifteen heavily armed riders. Clearly their leader, the man had a moonish face sunburnt and peeling, with gooseberry eyes squinting above an eagle-beak nose, and a cowcatcher jaw set at a truculent angle. He wore a dirty hickory shirt, and his dusty corduroys were tucked into the tops of fancy-stitched, high-heeled boots. The plain walnut grips of two revolvers protruded from his worn leather holsters.

"Tornado Turnbeau," Whittaker said with a dry chuckle. "He's fetched his kangaroo court jury. How do we plead, pardners?" As if answering his own question, the white-bearded old rascal raised his rear sight to the last notch and shot three times. Two of the riders wobbled drunkenly in their saddles.

Jessie and Ki had picked two of the nearest gunmen. Their carbines cracked almost in unison, and both those riders dropped their weapons as their scared horses lunged and whirled and stampeded.

The attack stalled, retreated to cover out of range.

Whittaker, Jessie, and Ki waited some more.

The moon began rising, big and round and yellow, even as the sun dropped behind the hills. That was in the defenders' favor, for this was a siege. They had grub, water, and plenty of cartridges. Below was feed for the horses and a big whiskey barrel filled with fresh water. That water might have a whiskey taste, but Whittaker swore his sorrel wouldn't drink any other kind of water. And Jessie's and Ki's roans had better learn how.

If it was a siege Turnbeau wanted out yonder, he'd get it. The log barn was out in the clearing. Anybody coming to it from the brush had a good twenty-five yards or more of open ground to cross, in case they wanted to set fire to the barn. "Let 'em try their damned arsenic tricks tonight!" Whittaker protested.

"It's called arson."

"Arsenic er arson . . . See that jasper?"

Whittaker's old Peabody cracked. A man who had been skulking along the edge of the brush let out a sharp yelp and went down on his hands and knees, then rolled over, doubling up and moaning. Whittaker fired again, and the man straightened out and rolled over on his back.

Turbeau's gang tried to set fire to the barn three times during the night. Each time the three in the hayloft spewed lethal lead and the would-be arsonists fell dead there in the moonlit strip. As Jessie commented after the third time: "That'll discourage them some." Then, just before daybreak, with the moonlight white, one of those freak winds started. It was just a breeze at first, then it gained strength. By shortly before dawn it was one of those strong river winds.

"Looks like we rode our luck," Jessie said. "We better get saddled. This will smoke us out."

Whittaker and Ki knew what she meant. Out there were a lot of dry branches and old logs that would burn like tinder. The big sparks and jets of flame would creep along the grass to the barn and, with the strong wind behind them, burn the barn and everything in their path.

"Let's beat them to it," Ki said. "White Water, have you got Tornado Turnbeau spotted?"

"He's in behind the outhouse. You know where Rufus is located?"

"I heard him hollering his orders," Ki replied, "from behind a brush patch. We've managed to keep him bushed-up there."

"Then we know where we're going?"

"I know."

"I could cover you and Miz Starbuck, if you'd try for a getaway."

Jessie responded to that one, her voice flinty. "I didn't come here to run away with my tail between my legs."

"If'n that's the case, if you'd have a last drink with me . . ."

"A drink." Jessie lifted the jug. "But not the last, partner."

Then Ki slid back the bar on the barn door. He swung into his saddle as Jessie mounted her roan and Whittaker settled astride his sorrel. Outside, some of Turnbeau's gang had just fired the brush, and the first angry glow of it was melting the shadow of the night. Ki leaned from his saddle and yanked open the barn door. Whittaker kicked the big sorrel in the flanks and grinned as the ornery horse laid its ears back, kicked out with both hind feet, then went out the barn door like a streak, its bewhiskered rider gripping his gun and cussing.

Jessie and Ki spurred their roan geldings and fled the barn on a dead run.

White Water Whittaker pulled his reins. Whatever he had been, regardless of past sins, he cleaned his slate now. He was yelling and cussing, as he slid that cantankerous sorrel to a halt out there in the open. He had a jug in one hand and his Peabody in the other, and snarled his challenge to all the enemies he had this side of hell. His voice was like thunder.

"Show your guts, you thievin' yaller-livered skunks! Come out and fight, you mangy, snake-eyed, lurkin' dregs of a laundry tub full of hawg lard! White Water Whittaker is declarin' hisself! Come out in the open, Turbeau! Don't die like a pusillanimous, snivelin' tinhorn whelp!"

Guns were cracking and bullets whining around their ears, so Jessie and Ki caught only fragments of Whittaker's rasping challenge. Cutting quick glances over their shoulders, they saw Whittaker making a target of himself and his horse to draw the gunfire, and knew that the old renegade out there was throwing away the life he loved as well as the next man. It was something mighty splendid—and suicidal—and there was nothing they could do to stop it. They had raked their horses from shoulder to flank, and there was no way of halting those big roans now until their race was won.

They crashed headlong into the covering brush. Then, of a sudden, Ki's horse stumbled and turned over. He kicked both feet out of his stirrups, hit the ground rolling, and came to his feet targeted by Rufus.

"I got 'im!" Rufus was bawling to two gunmen siding him, his revolver leveling for a point-blank shot. The revolver barked deafeningly. But the bullet missed, angling wide to the left. Rufus was collapsing on the ground, choking and gasping, a star-shaped disk protruding from his throat.

The two gunmen with Rufus jumped apart, while Ki tried to figure out which one to hit next. The bigger man leapt for cover. The second was slower, looking stupidly at Rufus thrashing around on the ground, then crouching and bringing his pistol to bear. Ki, with a whip of both arms, released two more *shuriken*. His right one slashed high into the abdomen, and his left, better placed, sliced like a scapel between two ribs and imbedded itself in the man's heart. The gunman crumpled atop of the throat-slit Rufus.

"You shit!" the third man yelled. "You goddamn shit!" Concealed from view behind a low-growing thicket, the man snapped off a hasty shot.

Ki was already diving aside. A geyser of dirt spurted close to his left foot. But that lightning flick of gunfire was all he needed. Even as the sound of the blast was still reverberating loudly, he was straightening, one of his daggers balanced in his hand. He threw, aiming carefully at where he'd glimpsed the muzzle flash.

There was a growl, a thrashing of brush, and the big bulk of the man's body jerked erect, then lunged aside. Ki, fishing a second knife out of his vest, tossed again. He heard another cry, the sobbing intake of breath, and saw the man reeling disjointedly before sinking out of sight in the brush.

Jessie, oblivious to her own mortal danger, had dismounted and was running on foot back toward the barn.

Luckily, opposing gunfire from Turnbeau's gang was lessening rapidly. Seeing the casualties pile up at an alarming rate, the gunmen were quickly losing interest in pressing the attack, and were retreating on horseback, their guts gone and their fighting finished.

A heavy-shouldered white-bearded man on a big sorrel rode out slowly from behind the outhouse, a smoking rifle in his hand. His shirt was crimsoned, and a bullet had nicked his cheek. Under bushy white brows his slitted green eyes glittered coldly. "Tornado Turnbeau's lyin' dead back there. I guess that helped speed them cash-fer-killin' weasels on their way. You two awri'?"

"We're all right," Jessie answered. "You hurt?"

"Nuthin' a gallon o' my likker won't heal—*pardner!*"

★

Chapter 9

Armed with permission from White Water Whittaker to bridge the Blister River at his crossing, Jessie and Ki rode back to Parthenon. There they returned their horses and caught the next eastbound stage to Lobos. When they arrived, Peck Adams was pacing outside the door of the depot, glowering fretfully.

"Didn't get back to town much sooner'n you," he declared, as they stepped from the stage. "First thing I find out, the Calexico mail run hasn't come in. I could be sore with you, Jessie. Things were going okay. At least they left me alone."

"It's nice to see you again, too, Peck. Who're *they*?"

"Tornado Turnbeau's gang."

"I doubt that. Turnbeau's dead. Besides, they wouldn't raid a mail coach," Jessie exclaimed. "That's federal property."

"Wal, then, mayhaps injuns raided it. Mayhaps some bast—er, bad man bought 'em whiskey and pointed out where to knock it over. I'll give it till tonight," Adams said. "Then I'm going out. No freight's come in, either. I don't savvy it."

"Could there have been a washout?"

"Been no storm," Adams said. "Dagnabit, I've got good drivers. They know the trail and're used to handling a stage. Takes considerable savvy to manage a six-hoss team up atwixt them buttes, where the trail curves round cliffs and the whole shebang could drop hundreds of feet into arroyos. The route here from Calexico has its bad bits of travelin'."

Jessie and Ki were inclined to agree, recalling the trail to the west, where overhanging cliffs towered on one side and but a few yards distant the crumbling lip flung off into nothing at all.

They walked to the hotel, and entering the lobby, they chanced to encounter Rita Hodge at the front desk. She was dressed for traveling and had a suitcase with her, and she was counting money into the hand of the desk clerk when they approached. Flushing a bit upon seeing them, she was not as demonstrative as the last time Ki had seen her, but cordial enough that no bystander could have detected her uneasiness.

"I'm leaving," she told them. "There's a train going to Calexico this afternoon, and I'm going to be on it. My father and I . . . Well, we've had a difference of opinion, and I simply can't take any more of this. And it's gotten worse. It's become a killing game."

Jessie asked, "What do you mean?"

"If you want to hear news first, you should set up your office in a hotel barroom. I was having a bite to eat in the dining room when a freighter went into the bar not more than fifteen minutes ago. I overheard him say there'd been a slide on

Battlement Ridge. A stage was wrecked—"

"Adams's mail run from Calexico!"

Rita nodded. "I suppose so. Anyway, they'd dug the stage out when this man started in. The passengers and mail are being taken to a relay station to the east of there. Probably there by now. No one killed, blessedly, but it certainly wasn't for lack of trying."

"It could've been a slide," Ki suggested.

"It would be the first in six years. Do you think it would happen at the very moment the coach ran under an overhang? It was luck that nobody was killed. But it won't be luck if the coaches don't run for a month."

"Yes . . . Yes, I think I understand," Jessie said. "A two-week delay of mail and passengers would jeopardize Peck Adams's mail franchise. In post office circles, slides aren't considered a valid excuse. But Rita, are you saying you think your father is somehow responsible for this?"

"I don't know what to think. He's never admitted anything of the sort. On the other hand, he's made it plain that he's determined to get the stage line. If Peck Adams lost a lot of customers and money due to accidents, and then lost the franchise, I wouldn't be surprised if Father offered to buy out your investment in the line." Rita glanced from Jessie to Ki. "You could thank me."

Ki said soberly, "I'm obliged. So is Jessie. But you'd be better off to let us find things out for ourselves. Your father might well find out about you telling us."

"I'd take the risk, Ki, if I thought it was worth it."

She was a tender-lipped, provocative woman, obscurely exciting. Ki studied her for a moment, running fingers through his hair, before he told her, "It isn't, Rita. It was over before it started."

She picked up her suitcase. "I can't say you didn't warn me, can I?" She started for the lobby door with a parting comment: "But don't look for any more favors from me, because even flounces don't make a girl *that* much of a fool!"

Jessie stared after her. "I don't know what to say, Ki."

"Then don't say anything," he replied tersely.

They quickly checked into their rooms, then left the hotel and returned to the stage depot. This time they found Peck Adams in a shed collecting picks, axes, and shovels. In a black mood, Adams said, "Rita Ballard, I mean Hodge, just came by an' tol' me about the slide. Tarnation! Man gets in the clear, and the next day a thousand dollars' worth of rocks falls on him!"

"Going out now?"

"Soon as I scrape up a road gang."

Shortly, workmen began to assemble in the stage yard to load packmules and crawl onto wagons. When at last they were ready to pull out for the stage wreck, Jessie and Ki saddled a couple of horses from the depot and joined Adams.

Four hours out, they broke for the Battlement Ridge grade. The slope of the butte was steep, climbing by rims to blunt, plateau-like peaks. About a half mile from there, they came upon the slide. It buried the road for a hundred yards, a flood of huge gray boulders, earth, and scrub.

Leaving their horses, Jessie, Ki, and Adams climbed across the rubble. They found the dead team at the lower fringe of the slide. The coach had been removed, apparently still capable of being rolled, but the horses had been dropped and half-buried by the stones.

Jessie stood looking back up at the slide. "How long?"

"Two weeks," Adams estimated. "The mail's going to have to go around the other side, by pack train. Any longer'n that will break my franchise. We'd be washed up!"

Adams took charge of setting up the camp. Because of the precipitous nature of the terrain, camp was made on the road itself. Messes were arranged, and as the pup tents went up, he started the first ragged gray stones rolling downhill. Presently, when matters were fairly well in hand, he walked with Jessie and Ki up the road, out of the dust and litter of the camp. From that vantage point they could see where a long, sun-blasted valley lay along the base of the buttes. Adams pointed to the far edge of the valley, where they could just barely spy the relay station in a grove of cottonwoods.

"I reckon the stage was rolled down to the station," he said. "The passengers may still be there, too, but I doubt it. Chances are they've been wagoned back to Calexico. Guess I'll have to ride down there and—"

There was a sharp, concussive powder blast at a distance. They glanced down the grade, Adams growling, "I didn't authorize no shot." But they did not see the dust, and a moment later, as the echoes poured back from the buttes, they heard a patter of small stones. There was a frozen moment of standing there, listening, and searching, and then Jessie's sharp question:

"Are they blasting above us?"

They looked up the rough staircase of rimrock ledges mounting to the top of the butte. A brown-gray island of rock and parched vegetation two hundred feet above seemed to be leaning toward them. Then they saw a giant block of granite separate itself from a buttress, like a keystone, and go into a slow fall toward the road.

The moment shattered. Jessie turned to run, but a sharp pain struck her foot and she fell. Ki swept her up in his arms and lunged toward the slide, hearing his own voice yelling something to Adams. Down the road, workmen looked around, resting on their shovels. Then they, too, began to run deeper into the slide.

A fragment of a rim high above the road had torn loose. Powder smoke drifted into the sky, and boulders were bounding down the steep hillside in a tawny fog.

Adams, sprinting beside Ki, tried to help with Jessie. A patter of small stones fell, and then a boulder hit the road with an impact that trembled the earth. Bounding away, the boulder struck a mule and carried it over the side. Ahead of Ki, dust blossomed in small spurts from the road. He stumbled, almost dropping Jessie. Recovering, he put her over his shoulder in a rude fireman's carry. Her hands clutched him as he ran on. Stones were landing in the old slide. A skinner deserted his team and in panic dove over the edge. Picks and shovels blocked the narrow cut. Adams shouted something and swerved away as, with a grinding roar, the main body of the blast struck the grade. A grating rattle of tons of disturbed rock thundered across the roadbed. A stone ricocheted into Ki's back. Again he tripped, and this time he crawled against a boulder near the bank and crouched there above Jessie.

After a long time the surflike roaring ebbed, became a dusty silence broken by the occasional pounding descent of a rock. Then it was over.

Ki sat back. Up the grade, the old slide had merged into a new one. Dust drifted over the rubble. Half-buried, a mule could be seen raising and lowering its head. A desert-gnarled tree lay, roots up, across the road. Jessie, beside Ki, was gray with dust, her hat hanging by its cord and her golden-red hair in disarray. Ki helped her up, just as Adams came out of nowhere, shirtless and furious.

"It was a shot," Adams bellowed, "wasn't it?"

Ki nodded. "He'd be up on the rims."

"Not unless he's crazy," Jessie countered. "He'd have cut a half-hour fuse and taken off for wherever he'd come from . . . probably Lobos."

"Maybe so, maybe not," Ki said. "And maybe we can pick up his trail and track him back to *who*ever he came from."

The rope line of saddle horses was restive. Jessie, Ki, and Adams tightened cinches, and mounting, they headed up toward the point of the blast. Near Battlement Ridge summit, a trail split east, winding from the butte down into harsh flatland country. Ki turned his horse down this trail. As Jessie followed, Adams shook his head.

"It's solid rock hereabouts," he protested. "You can't make me believe you can find any tracks to show some hombre headed thisaway."

"You're right, I can't," Ki agreed. "But there's a puddle of horse urine that hasn't dried out yet, and a cigar butt that's been freshly discarded."

After a moment, Adams grunted and came along.

They worked slowly eastward against a warm breeze off the buttes. The growth was scant, of tough desert scrub, dried grasses, and patches of squaw-carpet. Hillsides fell off into arroyos, arroyos led them along dry floodbeds, and then they would strike a switchback angling to a ridge a little lower than the last. Adams had his rifle resting across his saddle; suddenly his fingers pressed around the loading lever.

"See him?"

"Yes, just now," Jessie said.

About a mile away a horseman was working in and out of mottes of boulders. He was heading in the direction of Lobos, but in a very roundabout fashion, as if to throw off anyone trailing him, or simply because he wasn't sure of the route. After watching his circuitous riding for a few minutes, Adams gave a snort.

"We can come to a meeting with him, if he don't see us first."

Adams knew the country well and led Jessie and Ki on a more direct route that cut across a series of knolls. Finally they came to a small hollow below a steep and narrow canyon. "And unless I'm a heap mistook," Adams said, "it's from this canyon that the rider hasta come to reach town."

They drifted to within a hundred yards of the mouth of the canyon, which was screened in gray serviceberry. Ten minutes passed. A buzzard wheeled above them. Abruptly Jessie's horse turned its head to gaze upcanyon. A moment later a splotched cow pony, flecked with lather, pushed dispiritedly into view. The rider was a compact man in a plaid work shirt. He held a browned carbine in his right hand, watching the trail closely as he rode. Gashes striped the flank of the horse where a small-roweled spur had raked it. He could have been any ranch hand or laborer coming in from hunting meat, but the horse carried saddlebags too large for ammunition and too small for much equipment. They looked to Jessie about right for black powder and fuse.

She raised her carbine; the horseman twisted suddenly in the saddle and saw her, and Jessie saw the man's gun swing and had a darting glimpse of a brown, fat face before the gun erupted.

Earth exploded between her and Adams. A slug screamed away. Jessie's horse spooked, pitching and fishtailing. She could hear Ki and Adams yelling at their horses, and a hard rattle of gravel came from the canyon mouth. She turned and saw the cow pony buck-jumping uphill into the boulders. She fired a shot over the man's head and shouted at him.

Ki brought his horse under control. He shouted at Jessie, "Go with Adams, and the two of you cut him off from Lobos! I'll take after him!"

Goading his horse up into the boulders, Ki took to the slope, driving on a tangent between the canyon mouth and Lobos. Here and there were scrawny trees, like islands on the stony hillside, which ascended steeply to the crest of another butte. A rider could be flushed from cover in an hour's time. We've got him, Ki thought; but having a tiger in a sack did not amount to capture. The man did not know but what he was being sought for murder. He would not surrender with his hands up.

It was suddenly quiet. Ki reined in . . . waited, eyes and ears peeled . . . Then there was a rattle of hooves and he urged his horse forward. The hoof sounds halted. Ki's hand brought his horse in sharply. Through the scraggly growth he could see a long dike of sandstone lying across the slope like an arm. There would be no riding a horse across it to higher ground. It would be west, to the canyon; or east, to Lobos, and capture.

Ground-reining his horse, Ki walked quietly through the sparse stand of trees. After a few moments he heard a horse moving, and he pressed against a boulder and again waited . . . The cow pony came into view; Ki had a sick instant of trying to keep himself from firing at it instead of the rider. But as it came forward through the scrub, he saw that it was riderless, its reins tied to the horn.

Ki began to run. He slanted through the boulders and trees toward open ground, hearing a man moving. Then it was silent again. Ki slowed. He was walking carefully down an aisle of cinnamon-colored rocks when he heard footfalls on stone. He came out the other side of the clump of trees and saw the man sliding into a deep groove in the sandstone: It appeared that the stone had been sliced and the wedge removed like a center slice of bread. A man could just squeeze himself in there like a wounded fox and lie low . . .

Gunflame lanced from the crack; a report crackled through the air. Ki dropped flat, losing sight of the man, and backed into the trees for cover, then began to run. The slot was wider at one end than at the other from farther west, it provided no shelter at all. Ki had a view of clothing and gunmetal. The rifle roared again, and rock shards sprayed from a ricocheting bullet ten feet ahead of him. Ki hit the ground.

Then he took his time. The man in the slot was perfectly visible. He himself was screened by scrub brush. He was too far from the man to use his knives or *shuriken,* however, so when he reached the cover of a boulder, he made sure he had a shell in the chamber of his saddle carbine. He chanced a long look. The man was trying to climb. Where the fissure squeezed in, it was possible to scramble higher and make it to the next step of rimrock.

Ki shouted, "Dead or alive, mister!"

The man writhed and the rifle came to his shoulder. But Ki's carbine had driven its yellow flame out, and the echoes of it slammed back with a force that made him wince.

The rifle rattled down the rocks. The man began to fall, but he caught halfway down and hung there, head down. Ki could see the blood dripping from the tip of his nose. Lowering his carbine, Ki shook his head and then got up and went back to his horse.

Drawn by the gunfire, urging their mounts on in frantic urgency, Jessie and Adams caught up with Ki a moment later. Then they went to retrieve the body of the gunman, which took a measure of time. When they finally got the man down out of the sandstone fissure and onto the ground, Ki checked his pockets for identification and other clues. Not surprisingly, he found nothing.

"B'gawd, I know this feller," Adams exclaimed, peering closer at the man. "Not his name, exactly, but I seen him around. Works for Nimitz, Gallagher Nimitz."

"Who's this Nimitz?" Jessie demanded. "What's he do?"

"Just about anything that'll fetch him a dollar or two," Adams replied. "Lately he's been hauling cross-ties out to end-of-tracks for the railroad. Sure, that's where I've seen this jasper, on Nimitz's old freight wagon."

"Well, maybe someone in Lobos can supply his name."

Having roped the body behind Adams's saddle, they set off for town. After a long while, it occurred to Jessie that Adams had hardly spoken the entire time. The silence began to disturb her.

"What's wrong?" she asked him. "What's on your mind?"

Adams sighed wearily. "Oh, I reckon that second slide knocked the stretch out of me. Up to then, you couldn't have given me a railroad. I've put thirty years into proving that anyplace you could take a horse, you could take a Concord. But all of a sudden it don't matter much whether you can or not. Nobody gives a damn, if there's a smoke-belchin' monster to ride instead."

Jessie smiled. "That's likely me talking, thirty years from now. Somebody will come along with a transcontinental line of balloons, and you'll have to pay people to get them onto a train. But when it happens, I hope somebody trades me balloon stock for railroad stock."

"Yeah, I guess in a sense that's what you're doin' for me." Adams chuckled ruefully. "Hafta 'fess, though, I'd give your whole offer away if I could go back and start my first line again. That's the way of us stagers, Jessie."

Dusk hung over the desert town like smoke as they rode in. Lights were coming up behind dusty panes, mothers screeched after children, and a work crew from the railroad was hitting the saloons. Sheriff Zeigler was found breaking up a fistfight in a dance hall. Shown the body of the gunman, Zeigler confirmed that the man worked for Gallagher Nimitz, but said he couldn't recall ever hearing the man's name. Jessie and Ki told the sheriff what they knew—mostly repeating Adams's account—and then left Adams with Zeigler to make the detailed, official report.

They walked across to the train yard, where they located Otis Delivan alone at work in his private coach. Briefly Jessie sketched the events since they'd left Lobos for Blister River.

Pleased as he was to hear that she'd gained permission for a right-of-way from White Water Whittaker, Delivan couldn't help hiding his deep concern over the sabotage of Adams's stage line, "which smacks closely to what's happenin' to us," he told them. "While you've been gone, there's been another explosion out at the end o' the line. Blew an engine and a crane off the track. Killed two men and hurt a-plenty others. How the powder got planted there is a puzzler. There's a night shift workin' there at the railhead—men 'round at all hours. But it was done. She cut loose just as the engine was pullin' the crane into position, and now there's nothin' but a big hole in the ground. It was all the foremen could do to get the hands back on the job, and they're just pickin' at things. Scared to hit a real lick. But I swear, Tornado Turnbeau ain't broken us yet—and he ain't gonna."

"How can he? Turnbeau's dead," Jessie countered. "His gang is leaderless."

"Tell that to my boys," Delivan retorted.

"Could be that Turnbeau's only been acting as a front man," Ki suggested, "or perhaps he took in a partner, someone with whom to make common war against the railroad, and who's taken over the gang now."

"Could be," Jessie said thoughtfully. After mulling for a moment, she asked Delivan, "What do you know about Gallagher Nimitz?"

"Nimitz? Not much. He's got good business savvy, with his fingers in more'n one pie—has an interest in the Belle of Lobos hotel, f'instance, as well as freightin' cross-ties for me. I can't see him mixed up with Turnbeau."

"The man who blasted us worked for him, didn't he?"

"A bunch work for Nimitz, casual laborers mostly whose backgrounds can't take much scrutiny. Nimitz's made 'em toe the line, though, and's done a good job of deliverin' cross-ties. Gettin' the contract to haul them ties for the road has paid off for him, okay. Of course, a year or two of delay in the line bein' built would work to his advantage—he'll have his freightin' business just that much longer—but I reckon the road will throw business his way whenever it can, and probably he's already figgerin' on movin' into other lines. Nope, I don't reckon Nimitz to lose much by the road bein' built, and you can bet your bottom peso he knows it."

"I wish I knew what Nimitz knows," Jessie said, mostly to herself. It came back to her, then, the advice by Rita Hodge: *If you want to hear news first, you should set up your office in a hotel barroom.* Turning to Ki, Jessie said, "If Nimitz is part owner of the hotel, he might be found there. In any case, at this time of night, there're places you can go and hang around that I can't. See if you can locate him, Ki, and keep close tabs on what he does and says."

"All right. And you?"

Now Jessie turned to Delivan. "We need to get out to rail's end as soon as possible. If my hunch is right, and with a little luck, we may be in time to prevent another catastrophe!"

★

Chapter 10

Leaving Jessie and Delivan, Ki headed for the center of town, in search of Gallagher Nimitz. A good place to start, he reckoned, was in the barroom of the Belle of Lobos. After all, according to Delivan, Nimitz owned a share of the hotel, which might make it a natural watering hole for the man. Moreover, Ki had run into Rufus and those other members of the Turnbeau gang there, and since Jessie suspected Nimitz of being in cahoots with the same bunch, it made sense to check the same buzzards' roost.

The barroom was crowded, and sporting more activity than when Ki last visited. In the smoky distance, a mirrored wheel spun and a girl cried the bets. A mechanical piano and drum roared through "When Johnny Comes Marching Home," and girls and railroad laborers shuffled behind a rope enclosure. At the heavy walnut bar, an impartial rail supported the boots of townsmen, ranch hands, and laborers, who slouched with dark yokes of moisture lying across their shoulders.

At a table near the slowly clicking wheel, Ki spotted Vernon Hodge. The dapper land promoter was sitting with a thick-set, salt-and-pepper-haired man and a full-bosomed girl in a ruffled dress. Walking toward them, Ki noticed the broad, creased neck rising into the tough, grizzled hair, the flat ears and massive shoulders of the man; and that he was clad in common teamster garb of plaid work shirt, tan pants, and low-heeled boots. He watched the pair talk, Hodge gravely amused by something the other man was telling him. Wandering, Hodge's eyes came in sudden collision with Ki's. Ki absently removed his hat, ran his hand over his hair, and replaced it, not moving his eyes from the speculator's face.

"Let's pay respects to Mis-ter Hodge," he murmured to himself.

He went down the line of cocked hips at the bar, turning out through the tables to lay a hand on Hodge's shoulder. Hodge twisted to look up at him.

"How's the land business?" Ki asked.

The other man's dark, sober face watched him, and the girl laughed softly.

Hodge smiled. "I remember you. The name's Ki, isn't it? You hang around Miss Starbuck all the time. Matter of factly, my business is booming, Ki. You can't go wrong investing in land, y'know."

Ki eyed the other man. "A satisfied purchaser?"

Somewhat startled, the man shook his head. "Nope, can't say I is. Nimitz's my name, freightin's my game. Say . . . I know you, too, Ki. Heard tell you kilt Tornado Turnbeau a coupla days ago."

"Afraid you've got me mixed with White Water Whittaker."

"Wal, you kilt somebody."

"One of Turnbeau's men, a gent named Rufus."

The girl, raising her drink, smiled at Ki. "If we'd been properly introduced, I'd ask you to bring me a scalp next time."

"It's Indians who scalp folks, Violet, not Chink—er, Orientals," Nimitz said, rebuking the girl. Apparently he hadn't intended to introduce her, but now he said, "Ki, meet Violet Mayflower."

Ki gallantly bent over the hand she extended. She was a bold and attractive blond girl—two-tone blond, Ki bet—somewhere in her twenties. She had a pouting lower lip and wore dangling gold crosses as earrings; Ki hoped she took them off when she worked.

"It may not be too late yet to get you a scalp," he said. "Any preference as to color?"

Her dark, humorous eyes went to his own black hair. "Black is nice," she said. " 'Black is the color of my true love's hair' . . ."

"Violet," Nimitz growled, "we've got business to talk." He put his hand on the back of her chair.

"How many men did you kill, Mist' Ki?" Violet asked.

"Can't rightly say."

"Your first?"

"Violet!" Nimitz snapped.

The headlong music of the piano had resumed. Ki looked at Nimitz but extended a hand to Violet. "I expect Miss Mayflower is off-limits to non-teamsters?"

As the girl rose, Nimitz said, "Sit down."

But she was coming into Ki's arms, her face tilted to smile at him. They moved away to the roped dancing enclosure. Ki saw Nimitz sitting at the table, staring at his drink, and Hodge saying something bitter to the speculator.

"Don't you care whether you live to be an old man or not?" Violet asked him. They elbowed into a pack of dancing girls and intent laborers.

Ki grinned. "Not if I can spend my youth like this."

Violet laughed softly. "You don't like my friend."

"I just met him."

"But," she pouted, "you dance with me to make him mad."

And to see what you know about him, Ki thought silently, saying: "Let's put it this way: If there were ten pretty girls in the room, and Nimitz was with one of them, I'd dance with that one. But I didn't expect to draw the prettiest."

"You know," Violet sighed, "I'd rather be lied to by a man like you than have a man like . . . Well, any other man tell me the truth."

"That makes two good liars in this couple, doesn't it?"

Violet let that pass, asking instead, "Are you married?"

"Not even a reg'lar girl."

"Need a regular?"

"Only for tonight."

"That's too bad. I could have any worker in town, and I don't mean suckers. I could even have a land speculator like Hodge, if I wanted him."

"Then what do you like about me?"

"Maybe I like the fact that they're both afraid of you—"

She gave a sudden gasp and tightened her arms around him. Ki moved to loosen her grip. But as he did so, a shadow fell across him from behind—and the thought flashed through his mind that he had behaved like a pilgrim, letting the girl distract his attention while someone else maneuvered behind him.

Faster than thought, Ki whirled to face the threat. But he was not fast enough. Something heavy and yielding struck his head with sickening force. He had a fleeting impression of the hotel manager, the man who'd complained about damages when Ki had fought Rufus here. The man was swinging a blackjack. Ki tried to dodge. He tried to change ground and press the attack himself. But he was off-balance and encumbered with the girl's imprisoning embrace. He was stunned from the first blow, and his muscles would not do his bidding. He saw the blackjack descending again—and could do nothing to avoid it. The jar of the second blow ran deep down his spine, and the spinning dance floor came up to hit him.

He was down then, and helpless. But he clung doggedly to consciousness. He had lost track of the girl and the manager with the blackjack, but he had vision of a face bending over him. It was distorted and out of focus, but he recognized it at once. It was Hodge.

"This man's hurt," he heard the land speculator saying, and the voice was as distorted and out of focus as the features themselves. "Take him to my quarters. I'll fix him up!"

Rough hands grabbed hold of him, raised him half to his feet, and dragged him toward the lobby and the corridors beyond. His stunned, sick brain comprehended in that moment the manner in which he would be taken care of in Vernon Hodge's room.

He tried to protest. But his voice struck even his own ears as an unintelligible, drunken mumbling. And he knew what the crowd would be thinking: an uppity Chink, no doubt drunk, who got fresh with one of the bar girls and got his comeuppance. He tried to struggle. But his bones and his muscles were water. They dragged him inside the room like a half-full sack of rags folded in the middle, and dumped him on the bed, and then they went away. The girl, frightened, looked at him, but someone pulled her away.

In a moment the face of Hodge was before him again. A glass was forced against his mouth, and the distorted voice sounded unreasonably loud in his ears again.

"Here," it said. "Drink this."

Instinct warned him as to the kind of drink Vernon Hodge would most likely offer him. He clenched his teeth against the glass and twisted his mouth away.

"All right," the man snarled, "so you'd rather have it this way!"

Ki saw the blackjack poised above him. With stark clarity, he saw it start to descend. It seemed to take forever to reach him. He never knew when it struck . . .

Meanwhile, Jessie and Delivan were highballing to rail's end. Upon arriving, they hastened to the shack used by the chief engineer as his office. A light burned within.

They entered without knocking. The nervous little engineer looked up from his desk, considerably startled as a determined young woman and the boss of the company loomed in the doorway. He stared for a moment before finding his tongue.

"Good evening," he said at length. "What can I do for you?"

"We noticed as we arrived," Jessie said, "that there are more than a dozen cars loaded with cross-ties on the siding. Those ties were freighted in by Gallagher Nimitz, weren't they?"

"Yep, his outfit," the engineer agreed wonderingly.

"Well," Jessie said, "I want those ties unloaded tonight, and spaced out on the ground so they can be given a thorough examination."

The engineer stared, as if firmly convinced that he was holding converse with a lunatic. "Why . . . why . . ." he stammered, and looked to Delivan for support.

"It's deadly serious, even though it may sound loco to you," Delivan told him. "Right now we have no time to waste. Get a gang together and start 'em unloading them cars. Get all the light you can—lanterns, torches. We've got a chore to do if this railroad is goin' to be completed. Let's move!"

Urged on by the promise of double pay and the following day off, the men chosen by the engineer turned out from their camp cars and went to work. The ties were unloaded and laid in rows. Jessie and Delivan examined them with meticulous care, one by one.

Hour after hour they labored, with barren results. The first rose of dawn was staining the eastern sky when Jessie uttered a sharp exclamation.

"Look at this, Otis! I believe we've hit it."

With the construction engineer holding a torch close, Delivan hunkered down and peered at the almost unnoticeable opening in the tie's surface some ten inches from its end. With the greatest care, Jessie inserted the point of a hunting knife and scratched. A gleam of metal rewarded her efforts.

"This is it," she said. "Just how it works, I don't know as yet, but we'll find out, if we last that long." She glanced up at the engineer hovering over them with the torch. "Tell your men to go back to their camp cars and to stay there. Post a couple of foremen to see that the order is obeyed. I don't want anyone within a couple of hundred yards of the shack that houses your office. Oh yes, and I'll need some tools—a saw, a light hammer, a plane, and a wood chisel will do."

"Hold on, ma'am! This ain't lady's work—"

"Any work a lady does is lady's work," Jessie retorted frostily.

The order was given. The wondering hands obeyed, shuffling off through the first faint morning light. Then, while the engineer sought the tools, Jessie and Delivan carried the tie into the office and deposited it on the engineer's desk. They moved all available lights close to the desk. By this time the engineer had returned with the requested tools. Jessie took them and laid them on the desk beside the cross-tie. Dismissing the engineer, she then turned to Delivan.

"All right, Otis," she said. "Now you toddle along with your men. If something should go wrong, this whole kaboodle will be blown into the next county."

Delivan swelled like a grizzly bear sensing a fight. He glared at Jessie. "You just try to put me out."

Jessie grinned, and patted Delivan on the arm. "Thank you, Otis. Very well, we'll take our chances together."

Handling the tools gingerly, they went to work. Jessie sawed off the end of the tie nearest the small aperture through which the gleam of metal could be seen, and found nothing. She tried again, a little farther along the oaken beam, with likewise barren results. A third attempt, however, an inch or so beyond the little hole, rewarded her with a sudden screech of the saw's teeth on metal. Delivan sucked in his breath and stiffened.

"Getting hot," Jessie remarked. "Somewhere between this and the far end we'll find it. Just about in the middle, I'd say. Bring the lamp closer and let's make a try with the plane."

A few minutes of work and the outer surface of the tie was shaved off, revealing the white, close-grained wood. Jessie laid the plane aside and carefully examined the smooth surface.

"Look," she said to Delivan.

Delivan, bending closer, could clearly see a fine line of juncture that formed a rectangle in the surface of the wood cleared of the rough outer fibers.

Jessie picked up the chisel and hammer. "Now comes the ticklish part." With a steady hand she fitted the sharp point of the chisel against the hairline jointure. With swift, sure strokes of the hammer she drove the chisel into the tiny crack. Delivan held his breath and clenched his hands until his nails bit into his clammy palms. Jessie dropped the hammer and levered on the chisel, putting forth more and more of her strength. A section of wood rise slowly from the main body of the tie. Higher and higher, until at one end an opening was revealed.

"Careful!" Delivan cautioned. "There's the fuse."

"And the cap," Jessie added. A moment more and she said, "And there's the charge. Look, it's wrapped in felt to prevent a chance jar setting it off. Now, let's see if we can figure how it works." She examined the device carefully, her brows knitting together as she leaned over the tie and sniffed sharply. "Creosote. The wood was soaked in creosote to expand the fibers. When the creosote finally dries out, the wood contracts, which helps make the thing work." She straightened her aching back and dusted the particles of wood from her hands. "Keep this locked up," she told Delivan. "It will be needed as evidence, when Gallagher Nimitz stands trial."

"Y'sure it's Nimitz behind this, are you?"

"One of them, at least. Nimitz was unknown to me until today, when that man who works for him tried to blow us all up. I'm sorry the man's dead, because he was our link to these explosions. But I'd already decided that whoever was responsible for the sabotage here wasn't any outlaw hiding out in the hills, like Tornado Turnbeau—although he and his gang had their part in it all. Anyway, the man worked for Nimitz, and Nimitz is a teamster with a freight outfit, and that helped tie him in to the wheel coming off the coach a few days ago. That was no accident."

"How'd you savvy that?" Delivan asked.

"Ki found the threads of the axle had been run backward so that the forward movement of the coach would loosen the nut, instead of holding it tight. On the level flatlands it didn't matter. Up the grade of the first slope, where the wheel would strain against the nut, it started coming loose. Then the downgrade and the turns of the cliff trail did the job. It was almighty smart, and took knowledge of rigs like coaches and wagons. We didn't want anyone to catch on that it wasn't an accident, and just a coincidence that Turnbeau's men were on the scene. But right then I knew for sure somebody was out to kill us—which Turnbeau had no reason to want—and that meant the same someone responsible for the mysterious explosions. I figured I'd have to look for just the same kind of a smart trick where the explosions were concerned. I should've caught on to the cross-ties earlier, when we were out here before and that car full of ties exploded. The explosion occurred inside the car, and could not have happened under it."

"Why?"

"The crater hollowed out was wide and shallow, not at all like the one left by the explosion beside the roundhouse in Lobos. That proved that the charge went off some distance above ground. When the engineer kicked that car of ties too hard, somehow or other the loaded tie got just the right kind of jolt to set off the charge packed inside it.

"But how was them explosions set off?"

"You can see here for yourself," she replied, pointing to the tie. "It's been hollowed out carefully, so carefully that the slab of wood we removed would fit back in place with the line of juncture practically invisible. The charge of black powder, capped and fused, was wrapped in felt to protect it against the jars incidental to handling the ties and spiking the rails to them."

"And the jolting of the trains rolling over the rails set off the charge," Delivan interrupted.

"Yes, but not in the way you think. The charge was so well protected that trains could have run over the ties till Judgment Day and not set it off." Jessie motioned for him to peer closer. "Here—you see? This steel pin is closely fitted into the hole that's bored here in the tie. The pin's slightly curved and set at an angle to the surface, and the head of it would come exactly under where the steel tie plate would be set under the rail."

"Why, naturally! Ties are of the same length, and are laid so's their ends are in line, so it was a cinch to figger where the head of the pin should come. The tie plate would be just touchin' the head of the pin. The point of the pin was a small distance from this here cap." Delivan, nodding, wiped his damp face. "As trains ran over the rails, the weight pressing down on the rail would tend to gradually force the tie plate into the wood of the tie. It would take time, but lookin' at old ties, you can see that the plates have been forced down into the wood quite a ways."

"To make matters more certain," Jessie explained, "Nimitz gave that part of the tie an extra heavy soaking in creosote, which tended to swell the wood fibers. The creosote would dry out slowly, and the fibers would compress. The tie plate would grind deeper and deeper into the wood, forcing the point of the pin down against the cap. Finally a time would come when the weight of a passing train would jam the pinpoint hard against the cap. The cap would explode and set off the charge. Simple, but very shrewd. *Why* Nimitiz was doing this is another question, and I'm afraid I don't have all the pieces to that puzzle."

"Well, we got enough of 'em to get back to buildin' a railroad. I gotta advise the engineer to first remove every rail that's been laid here and give the ties a careful lookin' over."

When they located the construction engineer and Delivan had given him his orders, the engineer declared emphatically, "I'll do that. And I'll keep the tie in my safe for, eh . . . for safekeepin'."

"You'll be hearing from me soon," Delivan told the man. "Remember, none of the men here are to be allowed to leave camp until after tomorrow. That's plumb important. I'm depending on you to see to it that they don't."

"Mist' Delivan, suh," the engineer replied, "folks who desire to retain their peace of mind are not negligent in obeying my orders. And Miz Starbuck, a pleasure meetin' you. Good luck."

Luck for Ki, unfortunately, had been anything but good. In Vernon Hodge's room at the Belle of Lobos hotel, Ki lay for what seemed an eternity of time in a world of fantasy. It was as dark as the depths of a coal-black sea. But strange forms came to him from the outer shadows; fantastic forms that had no meaning . . . that talked and laughed and went away. Once there was light, and rough hands took hold of him, slapping his face and shouting his name. But this, too, went away. After that there was the nothingness again.

It was sometime later that he was fully conscious of being alive. And it was still later that he felt any interest in the discovery. This was when Gallagher Nimitz and the girl, Violet Mayflower, came into the room, Violet carrying a smoky lamp. Through narrowly slitted eyes, Ki watched them approach the cot where he lay.

Nimitz came closer; Violet was a pace behind him, extending the lamp, and talking: " . . . and you have him, Gallagher. What I'm wondering is what are you going to do with him? If you'd listen to Vernon, you'd bury him out in the desert somewheres. If you let him go, the railroad will have the law over here, quick. Where would you be then?"

"Right where I want to be, sweetcakes," the freighter said, pinking her cheek in a gesture of intimacy. "Just 'cause Phibbs worked for me don't mean I knows about them explosions, and now that he got his fool self kilt, there ain't no connecting that powderman to me. Or me to Hodge. And with Turnbeau dead, too, there ain't nothin' tyin' nobody to nothin' no more. Hodge is just bein' an ol' lady, sweatin' about suchlike."

Violet shivered. "I'm not sorry that Tornado Turnbeau is gone. His eyes, I swear, seemed to send icicles right through me. I never could understand why Vernon had to do business with the likes of him."

"Same reason Hodge hires me. We git his job done for him. Of course, Turnbeau was different than the gen'ral scrub lot of owlhoots—different in that he had brains. He saw clearly that the comin' of the railroad would end his outfit, or reduce 'em to maverickin' outlaws with mighty slim pickin's to be had. He couldn't have stopped it, but if he could've gotten the railroad to steer clear of his territory—to build round south, the way Hodge hasta have to sell all his prop'rty—Turnbeau would've put off the day o' reckonin' a good long time. Now, me, I don't care what route the railroad goes, but the longer it takes 'em, the longer I haul for 'em and the longer this hotel rakes in dough. With Phibbs on my payroll, I had a nice deal worked out, but everythin' hasta come to an end sooner or later. When the railroad's through—straight through or round south—then you an' me, we won't have nothin' but pleasure, the rest of our lives. Unless—"

His eyes glinted suddenly, and the teamster's drawl turned hard and cold. His mouth twisted cruelly.

"Unless you and Hodge have it made up b'tween you to throw me to the wolves, after he's cleaned up on his land spec'latin'. An' since you been askin', you might as well know that's why I'm keepin' this monkey alive. Hodge tries any funny shit, I'll turn the bucko loose! He'll be meat-hungry by that time, with a story to tell and blood to spill!"

With that, Nimitz bent over Ki and pulled back his eyelids, one and then the other. He grunted and, after another moment, took Violet by the arm and left the room.

The stifling darkness filled the room again. But the encounter had revived Ki, making him conscious of the pain in his head. He sat up and cradled his face in his hands, and then moved his arms and legs, gratified to find that he had not been tied. He had to escape, to carry word of Nimitz and Hodge and their plot against the railroad—or better yet, find the bastards and square accounts by himself. Moved by that thought, he rose from the bed and groped along the wall toward a crack of light that marked the door.

The door opened soundlessly in his hand, and he was looking down the main corridor of the Belle of Lobos. A man was standing there, his back to Ki as he struck a match to light a cigarette. The edge of Ki's stiffened right hand swung down in a vicious half-arc. There was a crunching of bone and a squashing of flesh. His left catching the man as he sagged, Ki dragged him back through the door. He used a neck-pinch to make certain the man stayed out a good long time, then stepped out into the corridor, shutting the door behind him. Guided by the sounds of revelry from the barroom, Ki headed along the corridor, disdaining in his anger to tread softly. He crossed the lobby and stopped at the entryway to the barroom and looked in, in full view of anyone who cared to glance his way.

Neither Violet nor Hodge was anywhere to be seen, but Gallagher Nimitz sat with his back to the wall in a poker game, near the rear of the spacious barroom. Apparently his luck was cold, for he seemed disinterested and slightly disgusted with the game. Idly he looked up from his hand, glanced about, saw Ki standing in the entryway—and the skin on his face turned to dried gray parchment. It was as though Nimitz had suddenly caught sight of Death itself, waiting.

For a long time neither moved. Their eyes might have been the only thing alive. Ki's like burning coals. Nimitz's as quiet and bright as the eyes of a snake.

"Gallagher Nimitz," Ki called, heedless of the odds he faced, "when you had your manager cold-deck me, you bought into a no-limit game. You've had your deal, and you've placed your bet. Now, stand up, Nimitz, and play out your dirty hand. It's hard to kill a dog that won't defend himself."

All talk, all movement in the room had ceased abruptly. All eyes were upon the rigid, coldly furious man who stood in the barroom entrance. So they didn't see the muzzle of a shotgun push slowly through the crack of a door in the lobby behind Ki.

Ki didn't see it, either. But he saw the light of sudden desperate hope in Gallagher Nimitz's eyes. And Ki knew that there was death behind him. He knew that it would strike if he turned, and strike if he waited. So he did what seemed the best to do. He dropped suddenly to the floor, and twisted about to face the door.

The universe exploded behind him as he dropped. The lobby trembled and the air roared in agony. He felt the heat of the discharge on his head and face. But the charge of buck overshot his head by inches and splintered a suddenly abandoned table in the barroom, midway between him and Nimitz.

But this Ki noted later. At the moment, he saw nothing but a bearded face in the crack of the door, above the shotgun. The lobby still reverberated from the shotgun's report as the man's death-rattling scream pierced the smoky air. The man in the crack sprawled forward, the shotgun falling in front of him, throwing daggers protruding from his brisket and the bridge of his nose.

Ki turned, still on the floor. Through the dust that was choking him he could see that Gallagher Nimitz was at last on his feet. There was a revolver in his hand.

Nimitz at last had the odds he needed to play out his hand. And he was smiling. But the smile and the odds were not enough. Ki snapped off two *shuriken* in rapid succession from the floor. The freighter's smile stiffened into a grin and his eyes lost focus. Nimitz stood swaying a moment, his eyes as blank as uncurtained windows. There were two *shuriken* buried in his chest, severing his heart muscles. And a silver dollar would have covered them both. When he fell, he fell backward, as if pushed by an invisible hand.

The silence that dragged into the room in the wake of the shooting was as unnerving as the blast of the shotgun. It was shocked, uneasy silence. The crowd was still stunned. It had not yet reacted to the killing of two men in the space of two, maybe three, seconds. And that reaction, when it came, would spell either triumph or disaster for Ki. For, while he had won over unequal odds temporarily, he could not hope to cope with the crowd if it turned against him.

Along the far side of the barroom, a door opened and Vernon Hodge came out, evidently from some private office. His hard, comprehending eyes took in the scene quickly. From Gallagher Nimitz's body, his eyes went to Ki. And such cold, feral hate Ki had never before seen in a pair of human eyes.

The crowd watched Hodge expectantly. And he didn't disappoint them. Elbowing his way through, he walked to the nearest table and climbed up on it like a politico about to give a speech.

"You've all seen what happened here t'night," Hodge shouted, in a hoarse, husky voice. "You're maybe wondering why Gallagher Nimitz had to die. Well, I'll tell you! Gallagher, as owner of this establishment, held out for giving you boys a few pleasures out here, while you build this road. The company, Otis Delivan himself, warned Gallagher to pack up. He stayed on to give you a few of the things you would have back in civilization! Now Gallagher's dead! And the killer that murdered him in cold blood is a company man, a bodyguard for none other'n Miss Starbuck, who's backing the road! Are we going to take that laying down?"

The crowd shifted uneasily and eyed Ki narrowly. The knowledge of him as a "company man" shed new light on the slaying. The air suddenly was charged with hostility.

"If we let them get away with this," Hodge harangued, "inside of two weeks there won't be a saloon or dance hall open on the road. I say it's time to show them where we stand!"

The crowd stirred threateningly. And Ki saw his hard-won victory turning to defeat. He had killed Gallagher Nimitz, but Hodge was alive and well, turning Nimitz's death to his advantage. In a few more minutes, Hodge would have the mob on him, like dogs of the pack, but if he tried to flee, he would only precipitate the violence. Ki, like Hodge, knew the power of crowds. He also knew the power of whiskey. He attempted a strategem of his own.

"The M&SD isn't closing the Belle!" he shouted in a voice that carried above the rumbling of the crowd.

"The Belle of Lobos is reopening right now—under new management! The drinks are on the house! Barkeeps, set 'em up! Everybody drinks!"

The bartenders stared at him, more startled by that order than by the killing their employer. Whiskey sold for a dollar a shot at end-of-track towns, and was never given away. But Ki didn't wait for them to act. He brushed through to the bar and, going behind the counter himself, began setting out whiskey by the full bottle.

"Don't fall for that cheap trick!" Hodge, still on the table, shouted frantically. "It's only a dodge, boys! He's trying to wreck the place!"

But Ki's psychology was sounder. Such a bonanza of free drink was beyond the wildest dreams of anyone in the room, and it was not to be ignored. The reluctant ones were elbowed aside by the eager ones, and the crowd surged toward the long line of bottles on the bar. Grasping hands seized dollar-a-drink bottles and knocked the necks off against the counter. If half the contents spilled, there was plenty more. Those who couldn't reach the bar struggled jealously to wrest bottles from those who were more fortunate. One man grabbed an armful of the booze and tried to get away. A dozen hands seized him, and he disappeared from view.

The crowd was now pouring around the ends of the bar to attack the shelves themselves. Ki flashed a grin at Hodge, whose voice no longer could be heard, and let the mob take over. Chaos filled the jam-packed barroom.

The bar overturned before the surging crowd. The heavy counter canted into the high backbar behind it, and the liquor-laden shelves toppled forward with a prolonged, shuddering crash. Three burning lamps were knocked from their pendants. Their wicks spluttered and blazed brighter as the high-proof whiskey from countless broken bottles took flame.

In an instant the Belle of Lobos had been transformed into an inferno, with blue liquid fire creeping over the canvas and plank boards. Fire-eyed gnomes executed a fantastic *danse macabre* in the weird light, as with clothing and hair flaming, they sought to escape that fiery corner of hell.

Panicked now, the crowd swept through the lobby for the narrow front doors. That inadequate avenue choked up, and there was fresh shattering of glass as men leapt through windows to safety. Others could not reach the windows, and the flimsy walls bulged and burst under the pressure, releasing the pent-up flood with a sound like the crack of doom.

Ki stood a moment, appalled by the havoc he had wrought. He caught sight of Vernon Hodge running back through the door he'd entered—no doubt to some rear exit or window—and though the smoke and fumes made for eye-watering blindness, Ki thought he saw that Hodge had hold of Violet Mayflower by her arm. Pursuing, Ki fought through the smoke and heat. There was a sudden crackling and popping like gunshots as the fire enveloped the dry tinder of the paneled walls around the doorway, and he had to shield his face from the rushing of flames as he dove through to the room beyond. As he'd suspected, there was a window open along the opposite, outer wall. He climbed out, landing in a narrow alleyway, and hurriedly looked in either direction. Cursing under his breath, Ki sprinted along the alley to the rear of the hotel, searching the night beyond.

Hodge was nowhere to be seen.

Damn!

★

Chapter 11

Came morning, and the arrival of Jessie and Delivan from rail's end. They stood along with Ki and a crowd of rubberneckers, regarding the ruins of the Belle of Lobos Hotel. It was a fuming, charred heap. Amid the ashes and the remaining embers of beams and posts could be seen blackened iron bed frames, heat-warped spitoons, and the few ravaged articles that had once been useful possessions of the hotel guests.

"All our luggage and belongings—gone," Jessie observed with a sigh. "Nothing that can't be replaced, though. And I still have this." She reached into her pocket and brought out the strange half a coin Jimenez Linares had slipped to Ki. "This seems to've started it all, and I guess it's fitting that it's around at the end."

"Not quite the end," Ki said. "Hodge is on the lam."

"Probably to Mexico by now," Delivan said.

"Well, wherever he's hightailing, he'll show up sooner or later," Jessie predicted. "But he's no longer any threat to us. His plot has been exposed; the men he was in cahoots with, Turnbeau and Nimitz, are dead; and the others working for them will be scattering to the wind."

Ki shook his head. "I still want to see him get his due. Hodge has absolutely no scruples. Even sucking his own daughter into his scheme. I'm glad Rita isn't here to learn how rotten her father is."

"I'm just glad it's over," Delivan declared. "And over it pretty well is, don't you think, Jessie? Peck Adams and his stage line is on our side now, and White Water Whittaker has given us our right-of-way across Blister River."

"Yes, I imagine there isn't much reason for Ki and me to stay in Lobos now, Otis. I think after a day's rest and a chance to buy some stuff, we should be heading on." Jessie looked thoughtfully at the half a gold coin in her palm, then added, "But I don't think we'll go straight back home to the Circle Star. No, there's a detail I want to clear up before I can call it completely over, before I can truly say this coin is around at the very end . . ."

At dawn the following morning, Jessie and Ki bid farewell to Lobos. After riding arduously all day, hot sunset found them far to the southwest, high along an iron-backed volcanic ridge that looked like the backbone of some prehistoric monster. They sent their gaze about all of the vast, tumbled terrain that they could view from here, amazed, never having seen anything that quite equalled the rugged barrenness of this desert. If they had been set upon the moon, its terrain could have looked no stranger.

Ki's voice broke his thoughts as they topped the volcanic ridge. "The Cantina Cara Dura, Jessie."

He spoke with something almost like awe in his voice, and a glance was enough to show Jessie the reason.

Beyond this ridge, in a cuplike circle of vermilion cliffs, lay a green jewel of an oasis. And in the center of the green bowl stood the cantina. Built completely of colored blocks hewn from the cliffs surrounding the oasis, it was a sprawling, single-story structure that stretched out wings in all directions like the tentacles of an octopus.

"Linares," Ki's voice drew Jessie's attention again, "may've gotten tired of waiting for us, so perhaps he won't be looking out for us."

"If we're right in thinking he's at the cantina." Jessie frowned as she studied the building ahead. "Nothing I guess we can do except ride in, and trust we catch him off-guard. Once we lay hold of the slippery cuss, I'll sweat the truth out of him."

Their horses needed no urging down this last steep slant of the rocky road into the oasis. They went loping along at a fairly good clip, their mounts smelling water down there below. A stone trough, fed by a pipe from some underground spring, lay in front of the cantina's arched entry, and it was there they tethered the horses. A black, ancient door stood open. As they strode stiffly past it, Jessie read the legend stenciled in white against its upper rim: *This portal is never closed to those who seek solace.*

"What an odd greeting," Jessie remarked to Ki, "from the outlaw overlord of the desert here."

They moved the length of the short entrance hall and paused for a moment in a second archway to accustom themselves to the dimness of the main tavern room. Heavy shutters that looked as though they were never opened kept light from entering through any of the windows. It was as dark as if it were night. As their eyes grew accustomed to the dimness, they noticed the flat, low ceiling, and their admiration for the beauty of this cantina in the heart of desolation grew. The ceiling was made of beautifully cut slabs taken from the painted cliffs surrounding the oasis. A master stonecutter had set and matched the blocks so closely that only crisscrossed oaken beams were needed to support their weight. The floor was an example of expert flagstoning, but the rainbow hue of the stones was splotched here and there with odds stains that looked like rust. The stains spoiled the mosaic effect, but as their eyes focused on the bar beyond, Jessie and Ki forgot that one jarring note in the midst of this unexpected perfection.

Without thinking, they had been moving closer to the short, black bar that occupied a part of the tavern wall, and now they were close enough to see the fabulous coin collection of which they had heard so much. In panels that surrounded a wide central mirror, gold, silver, and odd paper banknotes glowed with a beauty of their own, beneath the cone of light cast by a single oil lamp bracketed above the collection.

"Look!" Ki said, pointing to the apex of the collection.

A gold piece occupied the collection's place of honor—the half of a once round coin. Its ragged broken edge, Jessie knew without looking closer, would join neatly with the segment in her own pocket. The sight was enough to make her forget railroads and stolen horses. And the man who came padding silently from behind a curtained opening at one end of the backbar completed the bewilderment that was flowing like water through her body. Nobody needed to tell her or Ki that they were looking at *El Cochino*. Jessie's stomach was as strong as most, but she could barely repress a shudder.

No description had ever exaggerated The Gross One's size. He towered almost seven feet tall, and most of his three hundred pounds seemed to have gone to belly—a great, swelling paunch that strained the seams of his thin white shirt. Above that quivering paunch his face was as white as his shirt. That in itself was a mystery. It didn't seem possible in the blazing heat of this desert country that a man's skin could remain so pale. His hair, too, was a bleached, ugly white. And then, as light from that single lamp above the bar struck the giant's eyes, Jessie saw him blink as though in pain. It gave her the answer to El Cochino's ugliness. The man was an albino!

Layered with desert dust, Jessie and Ki looked as wearily derelict as any hunted man who had sought refuge here. Their bedraggled appearance seemed to please the giant, for a smile moved his thick, rubbery lips as he brought a bottle and two glasses from beneath the bar.

"You two look like you could stand a drink," he said in a voice that was as deep-toned as a vibrating gong.

Jessie's brain was spinning with shock and more unanswered questions. How had the twin half of the coin in her pocket found its way into *El Cochino's* collection? Was there nothing more to this mystery than the desire by Jimenez Linares to sell the giant the rest of the gold piece? It looked to be the logical answer, and yet Jessie had the hunch that her guess was far off the right track. Of just one thing was she completely certain. Linares knew the answers. And on that basis she made her decision.

"There're times," she said flatly, "when it pays to be honest. Somewhere hereabouts is a wily thief named Linares, Jimenez Raul Linares, and we want to see him."

Soundless laughter had shaken the giant's paunch as Jessie talked. Ki noticed it. "What's so funny about what she's saying?" he demanded.

El Cochino's silent laughter changed to a deep-throated chuckle. "You bring the babe in arms no trouble?" he queried.

Taken aback by the giant's mild, almost gentle manner, Jessie blurted out, "Babe in arms?"

El Cochino shook his ponderous head. "He is but a babe in arms," he repeated. "A hidalgo, playing at being a badman. He came some few days ago, proclaiming himself a desperado, but I've handled far more badmen than you are years old, and I know the cut of them. Now, you two, for example, I'd size you up as straight and narrow. My Cantina Cara Dura is not the place for your kind."

Ugly though he was, Jessie found herself liking the innkeeper. "I'd take you up on that," she said frankly, "except that first, I've got a little something to hand that so-called hidalgo, and I plan to do it personally."

The giant's paunch was shaking again with that silent laughter. "Lady," he said, and his voice had grown softer, "I neglected to add that I expect some slight recompense for helping you find your man."

"Name your price."

"It is not your pennies I want. Perhaps the mere answer to a question will be recompense enough. When Jiminez Raul Linares entered my cantina, I watched his eyes swing to my backbar. It is the nature of my affliction, my frien's, that I see better in darkness than in light. Now, it was quite dark when Linares came, and I doubt if he realized that it was not hard for me to see which of my coins caught and held his attention. When you entered, my frien's, your eyes found the same coin."

There was danger here for them. Jessie could feel it like another presence in the room. She glanced once, sharply, at Ki, then turned back to the giant. "And what if we won't or can't tell you why?"

El Cochino spoke without the faintest change of expression. "You will remain here at the Cantina Cara Dura until you change your minds."

Jessie drew a deep breath. She understood now that the albino had been watching them through a crack in those curtains at the corner of the backbar, and had seen them pause at the sight of the companion piece to the coin in her pocket. From the very beginning, she had realized that they were playing this game blind. And she was getting tired of it. She made her decision, and with her left hand she brought the half coin she had delivered here from her pocket. Her right rose above the bar at the same time, and it held her custom pistol.

"This is what I brought to your Cantino Cara Dura," she said in tones that were as chilly as the steel of her pistol. "Linares was in a fight in a town called Flush, and he slipped this thing to us to save it, I suspect, from a hardcase named Bodeen and four henchmen of his. He told us to bring it here, and he stole our horses to make sure and certain we'd do it. So we've got half and you've got half. Get that piece down off the wall, and let's put them together. Maybe we can figure out a few answers."

El Cochino had reached one long arm back with unerring accuracy beneath the cone of lamplight, and his fingers, deft as a woman's, had plucked his half of the strange coin from behind its glass.

"I like you, lady," he was saying as he moved. "You are straightforward. You spoke of a man named Bodeen. It was one so named who sold me this odd piece in Los Angeles, perhaps six weeks ago. He is not the type of American of which our country can be proud. I understand he married into a fine old California family, and that they've been suffering ever since." The albino's fingers had fitted the two halves of the coin into a single whole. Against the dark wood of the bar, the gold seemed to glow with a light of its own. "This must be worth a-plenty *dinero—*"

"It is, señor." The voice came from the arched entrance to an open hall, in the wall of the room past the bar. "It is the key to the riches of Rancho San Fundador."

Jessie and Ki twisted around. They had heard no sound, but evidently the giant's ears were keener than their own, for he did not seem surprised at the sudden words. Jimenez Raul Linares stood in the opening, rubbing sleep from his eyes. He had discarded his floppy hat, but otherwise he was still garbed as a *paisano.*

"You have done well," he said, his dark glance touching Jessie. "And I am sorry to have caused you an' your amigo inconvenience, but you were how they say, neighbors, no?"

"Rancho San Fundador," Jessie said, almost as though talking to herself, so stunned was she by this development. "You're one of the heirs?"

Linares's thin face twisted bitterly. "I am the only *true* heir, señorita. Thees gringo *cabrone,* Bodeen, he was the husband of my sister, and claims an equal right. Were he to be the one to present the grant papers, the courts would honor his claim before mine."

Jessie's eyes had found the coin on the counter while Linares talked, and at last things were becoming clearer to her.

Linares nodded and explained, "The coin is a *mapa,* a map. To a man who knows the key, the lines upon the coin tell the hiding place of the old parchments. Many years ago the wise Don Fundador hid the grant papers in a place where no man might find them unless he possessed the key. And on the hammered coin of gold you see he engraved the map that would show the location of the parchments. Then he severed the coin, and half of it he kept himself, and the other half he entrusted to the care of my family."

"And Bodeen stole one of the halves?"

"*Sí.* After the death of the Don, recently, it was discovered that his half of the coin was missing, and suspicion pointed to Bodeen. The proof came when I learned in the gaming rooms of the Bella Union in *El Pueblo de los Angeles* that Bodeen had sold the half of the curious coin to Señor *El Cochino* here."

"So Bodeen was after you for your half, or to shut you up?"

"For both reasons, I believe. He learned the meaning of the coin, and he came to my hacienda with his three *coyoteros* to torture me into parting with my share of the coin. But I escaped him, and in the disguise of a peon headed for San Bernardino. On the way, in Flush, was where they caught up with me, and it was there I saw you, Señorita Starbuck. You are well known to anyone who reads newpapers and periodicals. Thus I recognized you and your amigo Ki. And I knew of your involvement with the Mexicali an' San Diego railroad venture, and your need for a right-of-way across the Fundador grant lands. The rest is simple. To insure my welcome here and to make certain that you followed with my half of the coin, I borrowed your mounts. Once here, I hoped that we could convince this good señor, *El Cochino,* that he could serve us by allowing us to match the halves of the coin. One look, amigos, is all I need, and in return, Señor *El Cochino,* I will present you with my half of the coin. Together, they should add much to your collection."

The soundless laughter had been shaking the giant's paunch while Linares made his earnest talk. Sight of it gave Jessie a little warning of what to expect.

El Cochino's rubbery lips twisted in the caricature of a smile. "A treasure indeed, that coin," he drawled. "Yes, my frien' Linares, but think of Rancho San Fundador. Ah, that would be the crowning jewel for the diadem of a prince. I think it will be I who will present the deed to the rancho in the Los Angeles land courts!"

As he spoke, one of his huge, pale hands darted toward the golden coin on the bar, but his fingers were not as swift as the downward strike of the gun that Jessie still held in her hand. Like a teacher cracking an unruly pupil's knuckles with a ruler, she laid the barrel of her Colt across the albino's hand. Blood started from the man's smashed knuckles.

Hatred, stark and savage, gleamed in the albino's odd eyes, and his hand jerked back like the head of a serpent into its hole. He took one ponderous step backward, and his bloody-knuckled fingers started toward the heavy carved molding at the base of the collection.

Jessie's free hand was on the bar, reaching to scoop up her—or rather, Linares's—half of the coin, when a voice struck out at them from the gloom of the arched entry hall.

"Touch it and you're dead, Miss Starbuck!"

Jessie instantly recognized the voice of Vernon Hodge. Her initial reaction was one of shock, but the next instant she realized she shouldn't be surprised by his presence here—the Cantina Cara Dura, after all, was a way station for wanted men on the lam, and Hodge certainly fit that bill. Knuckles white about the grip of her pistol, which lay in her right hand along the bar, she moved only her head to look at Hodge. Ki, his lips slitted back from his teeth, stared defiantly at the land promoter, who stood poised with a revolver in his hand. Shadowy behind Hodge were three gunmen—one, spiderlike, was all big chest and little bowlegs; another had the intense, burnished eyes of a lynx; and the third was squat and muscular, his puff-lipped mouth open in a salacious grin.

"Your first shot better finish me," Jessie said flatly, "because if it doesn't, I'll get you."

As though his arm had tired, the giant albino had dropped his bloody hand to the backbar shelf below the lower rim of his coin collection. Both of his hands were in sight, and there was no sign of a weapon. Before Hodge could answer Jessie's challenge, *El Cochino*'s deep rich voice boomed affably. "Let 'em enter, Miz Starbuck. Gen'lemen, please come in. Why can't we all have a drink and talk this over sensibly?"

Jessie knew that *El Cochino* wanted the whole coin as badly as any of them. There was only one answer to his behavior now, she realized, and a feeling of unexplained danger that had nothing to do with Hodge and his gunmen crawled like droplets of cold water along her spine. If Ki sensed it, he showed no sign of it. Linares stood at the far corner of the bar, his face gone as pale as the old parchments for which he searched. He had one hand over his shoulder, fingers inside the collar of his loose blouse.

Hodge's eyes had found Linares. "You got a knife in your hand, greaser," he taunted. "But don't get the notion you can use it. I've got six slugs here that can travel a lot faster than a blade!" He came moving into the cantina proper as he spoke, flanked by his three companions. "I'm taking the coin. It's all I want. Get that, Miss Starbuck?"

Jessie drew a deep breath. "Yes. I get it." She did not believe it, though. Hodge wouldn't leave anyone alive, of that she was sure, and by the absolutely vicious way he was eyeing Ki, she knew the first victim to die would be the one Hodge held responsible for his downfall. Behind Linares, she glimpsed an open archway that no doubt led into one of the cantina's labyrinthine wings. If, Jessie thought, she and Ki and Linares could get the coin and themselves into that passage, they'd at least have a fighting chance to dodge pursuit until night would give them an opportunity to escape.

Hodge was drawing closer with short, cautious steps. For the first time he seemed to sense something wrong. "Move back from that gold piece, Miss Starbuck, and leave your gun right where it is."

Out of the corner of her eye, Jessie saw the albino's bloody fingers inching slowly up the wall of the backbar, toward the solid molding that edged the bottom of his framed coin collection. It came to her then, with certainty, that great danger for all of them lay just beyond the giant's crawling hand. She moved then, risking everything on the hope that Linares would be alert and ready to take advantage of any play she made.

"You can have my gun, Hodge," she said through clenched teeth, "when I get through with it." The barrel of the pistol swept sideward. She felt the gunmetal contact the gold coin, and she heard it slither the length of the bar and drop solidly to the flagstone floor at Linares's feet.

"Why, you bitch!" Hodge yelled, and his revolver chopped down to level on Jessie as another cry overrode his own.

It was the spiderlike man's voice. "Chief, *El Cochino*! Get him—" The gunman's revolver exploded as he spoke.

Jessie saw the giant's huge paunch shudder as lead drove into him, but the slug did not halt the powerful twist of the man's hand as his fingers closed over the molding at the base of his collection. The dark wood moved, and then sound dwarfed the roar of revolvers that filled the cantina. A mosaic block in the flat stone ceiling overhead dropped with a rush. Its weight smashed the gunman to the flagstone floor.

A hand caught Jessie's collar and yanked her backward. She felt Ki's breath against her ear, and heard Linares's voice from the end of the bar: "*Por Dios!* The roof is a death trap."

A keystone controlled by a trigger operated from that molding had been released at the giant's twist, Jessie realized. A falling block grazed her arm as she and Ki, and then Linares, reached the protection of the side archway.

Jessie took one last look at the Cantina Cara Dura, and she knew that she would never again forget the sight. Where Vernon Hodge and his gunmen had stood was a heaped pile of roof stones, colorful as a rainbow. If they had been cleared and those dead men buried, there would have been more of those odd stains that she had noticed on the flagstone floor upon entering. But this time that treacherous roof would not be replaced to hang above men's heads like a true shadow of death, for the murderous, sick brain that had conceived such a lethal device was just as dead as the foursome beneath the colored stones.

The spiderish gunman's bullet had avenged them. Hand only now slipping from the molding as death released its grip, the giant albino slid slowly down behind the fabulous backbar he had treasured more than life.

"Come on," Linares was groaning. "*Por Dios,* let us get out of this death trap. Perhaps it is just that such men should die, but that does not make my stomach feel any better."

"Nor mine," Jessie found herself murmuring. "From now on, I'm minding Starbuck business, which is normal, everyday business."

"Ah, but you will be granted your right-of-way across Rancho San Fundador, Señorita Starbuck, for your help."

Jessie smiled wryly at Linares, her tone a tad acerbic. "For which I thank you. Right now we're going to ride back to Lobos, and not just to arrange the right-of-way with Otis Delivan. No, sir, there's a certain feed and stabling bill for two horses that's owed the Shamrock Livery there. And, Señor Jimenez Raul Linares, I aim to see that you pay every red cent of it!"

Watch for

LONE STAR AND THE BELLWETHER KID

133rd novel in the exciting LONE STAR series
from Jove

Coming in September!